ELVISPRESLEY

ALL SHOOK UP

First Published by FHE Ltd

CAT NO: BZB0324

Photography courtesy Pictorial Press, Wikimedia
Commons, Getty Images unless indicated otherwise.

ISBN: 978-1-912332-01-4

contents

Contents

ELVIS IN THE BEGINNING THE INSIDE STORY

One Saturday in the summer of 1953, an 18 year-old Elvis Presley walked into Sun Studios on Union Avenue in Memphis, Tennessee and changed the world. He couldn't have known it at the time, but he was taking the first steps on a journey that would revolutionise both the music industry and popular culture and, in doing so, establish himself as one of the major icons of the 20th Century.

He was there to make a private recording of 'My Happiness', a 1948 country hit. He would later say that he wanted to make the record as a birthday present for his mother. Occasionally he would contradict himself, saying he just wanted to hear what he sounded like. But he had a burning ambition to be a singer, so he must have hoped that someone in Sun Studios would spot his talent and give him the break he craved.

That someone was Sam Phillips, the owner of Sun Studios and its retail arm, Sun Records. Phillips, a sharp operator, was always on the lookout for new talent and used the private recordings as an audition facility. He was an experienced record executive, recording almost exclusively black blues artists including BB King and Howlin' Wolf. He had released several sides to major R&B labels, including Chess Records, but what he really wanted was a hit for Sun Records. He'd had a local success with 'Just Walking In The Rain' by the Prisonaires, and 'Rocket 88' by Jackie Brenston and Ike Turner, widely regarded, in retrospect, as the first rock'n'roll record. But Phillips wanted more.

His dream was to find a white singer who could sing with the feel of a black singer. A white singer who could sing the blues. If he could do this, he believed, he would break down the racial barriers in America that shackled black artists just as surely as they had been by their slave-masters. In Fifties America, even the radio waves were segregated – white radio stations refused to play black 1 music, and black radio stations ignored white music. But if he could find a white man who could sing black...

When Presley walked into his studio to record 'My Happiness' and abortive version of the Ink Spots' song, 'That's When Your Heartaches Begin', which stopped abruptly, Phillips was intrigued. After Presley had left, he wrote in the studio diary: "Good ballad singer. Hold." Presley went back to his job in Crown Electrics and waited for the call back. But nothing happened so he went back into Sun to privately record two more songs. Six months later the call finally came. Presley would later recall that he was in the studio before the receptionist had put the phone down.

Sam Phillips got Presley to sing just about every song that he knew. Accompanying himself on a battered guitar, Presley obliged. His favourite artists were the Ink Spots and Dean Martin, so the songs were mainly ballads. After three hours, Sam called it a day. The results were inconclusive. There had been no 'Eureka!' moment, but Sam thought it worth going a little further.

He phoned Scotty Moore, a 22 year-old local guitarist who, with his band the Starlite Wranglers, had already had one unsuccessful release on Sun Records. Sam and Scotty were kindred spirits. Both were ambitious and both were searching for something different. Sam arranged for Scotty to put Elvis through his paces. A meeting was set up at Scotty's house, along with Bill Black, the Wranglers' bass-player. They spent an afternoon going through Elvis's repertoire, all ballads. When Elvis left, Scotty phoned up Sam with his verdict.

He wasn't overly impressed but admitted "The kid can sing." Sam suggested they try again, this time at the studio. Scotty asked if he should bring the Starlite Wranglers along. "No," said Sam, "just Bill."

The following night, they gathered at the studio. They wouldn't have realised it at the time but all the elements were already in place. All they lacked was the magic song. They spent the evening trying out different songs, still mainly ballads, but nothing clicked. Presley got more and more frustrated, thinking his chance was slipping away. Consumed by a sense of desperation, he began changing vocal lines and lyrics, searching for something that had never been done before. Still nothing clicked. From the control booth, Sam told them to take a break. It was getting late and there was talk about calling it a day. During the break Elvis suddenly started singing 'That's All Right', an old blues number by Arthur 'Big Boy' Crudup. Scotty and Bill joined in. This wasn't serious. This was just a bit of fun.

In the control room, Sam froze. This was what he'd been looking for. A white man who could sing black music. He was surprised that Elvis even knew the song, so different was it from the ballads that had gone before. Keeping his voice level, he told them to work out a beginning and an end so they could record it. Elvis, Scotty and Bill were surprised. They'd only been fooling around, but they did as they were told. They worked on the arrangement, guided by Sam, and stripped the song down to its basics.

Scotty, like many guitarists of the day, was a devotee of Chet Atkins, the doyen of country pickers. Sam told him to cut back on the Atkins style and find his own way through the song. Without a drummer, Bill's bass had to drive the song. Using a slap technique, he set up a fearsome, hypnotic rhythm that, along with Elvis's acoustic guitar, perfectly complemented Scotty's pared-back guitar. And over the top, Elvis's uninhibited voice soared into uncharted territory. Sam knew they were

getting close, so he started recording. A couple of takes later the song was in the can. None of them knew what they'd done. But one thing was for sure – it was certainly different. They'd just invented Rockabilly.

Hearing the song now, it can be difficult to understand the true magnitude of the achievement, particularly in this day and age when fusion music seems purely a matter of artistic choice. Put simply, it was a blend of country music and blues. But the communities from which these two styles of music came were socially polarised, especially in America's bible-belt South. Ten years before the Civil Rights Movement, it was racial dynamite. After hearing the playback a slightly embarrassed Scotty Moore said: "Man, when they hear this, they'll run us out of town." Elvis was dumbfounded. "I've never sung a fast song before," he said.

Sam needed time to think. He'd found what he was looking for but, having found it, didn't quite know how to handle this weird hybrid. He needed a second opinion. Later that night, he got it. Old friend Dewey Phillips, a Memphis radio disc-jockey on WHBQ, called in at Sun Studios in the early hours after his radio show. This was a regular occurrence.

Dewey, one of the few white DJs in the south who played black music, needed to wind down, and there was no better way to do it than have a few beers and talk about music with Sam. Sam played him the tape of 'That's All Right'. At first Dewey didn't know what to make of it either but, after repeated plays, fell in love with it. He promised to give it a spin on his show the following night, so Sam ran off an acetate for him.

Next morning Sam called Elvis to tell him he was going to be on the radio that night. As the time approached, Elvis, consumed by nerves, tuned the family radio to WHBQ so his parents could listen to the show, and went to the movies. Half-an-hour into the show, Dewey played 'That's All Right', and the WHBQ switchboard lit up. Legend has it that 47 calls came in immediately. Dewey played it again and again, at one point seven times in a row. He phoned the Presley home to get Elvis over to the station for an interview, but was stunned to find he had gone to the movies. "Get him over here as soon as you can," he said, as politely as possible. The Presleys went down to the movie theatre, found their son and sent him off to the radio station. When he got there he was rushed into the studio.

"Sit down, I'm gonna interview you," said Dewey. Elvis was shaking with fear. Sensing this, Dewey pretended to cue up a couple of records and started chatting to him, leaving the microphone open. During the conversation he asked him what school he had gone to. "Humes High School", came the reply.

Dewey made sure he got that in because, in the educationally segregated South, that told the listeners he was white. At the end of the interview, Dewey thanked Elvis. "Aren't you going to interview me," asked Elvis. "I just did," said Dewey, and put 'That's All Right' on the turntable again. Both men were ecstatic. During the show there had been upwards of five hundred calls.

Sam was delighted, but was already focusing on the next step. He had to release 'That's All Right' as a single, but they needed a B-side. He brought Elvis, Scotty and Bill back into the studios and, over the next few days, they tried out different numbers.

Once again a song emerged while they were messing around during a break. Bill started singing a speeded-up 'Blue Moon Of Kentucky', a beautiful country waltz that had been a hit for Bill Monroe & The Bluegrass Boys in 1946. Elvis and Scotty joined in and, suddenly, it clicked. It was almost a mirror image of 'That's All Right' – but, whereas 'That's All Right' had been a blues song with a country feel, 'Blue Moon Of Kentucky' was a country song with a blues feel. It was every bit as groundbreaking as 'That's All Right', but Sam put a more sophisticated tape echo on Elvis's voice and it dripped with atmosphere. It almost sounded as if it had been recorded outdoors, on a rainy night, in a field in Tennessee.

By the time the record was cut and released there were already advance orders for six thousand copies. They had a local hit. Sam sent promotional copies out to all the local radio stations who began featuring it heavily, most stations favouring 'Blue Moon Of Kentucky'.

Sam got Elvis his first gig, a guest spot at the Bon Air Club, a Memphis drinking club that featured hillbilly music. Scotty and Bill were gigging musicians and took it in their stride, but Elvis was a mass of nerves. They only did two songs, both sides of the record, and the reception was unremarkable, but Sam was impressed with Elvis's stage presence. Elvis thought he had failed. The next gig was a bottom of the bill spot supporting Slim Whitman at Overton Park, on the outskirts of Memphis. The first-night nerves of the Bon Air gig were compounded by a much larger crowd and Elvis almost froze.

Man, when they hear this, they'll run us out of town.
Scotty Moore

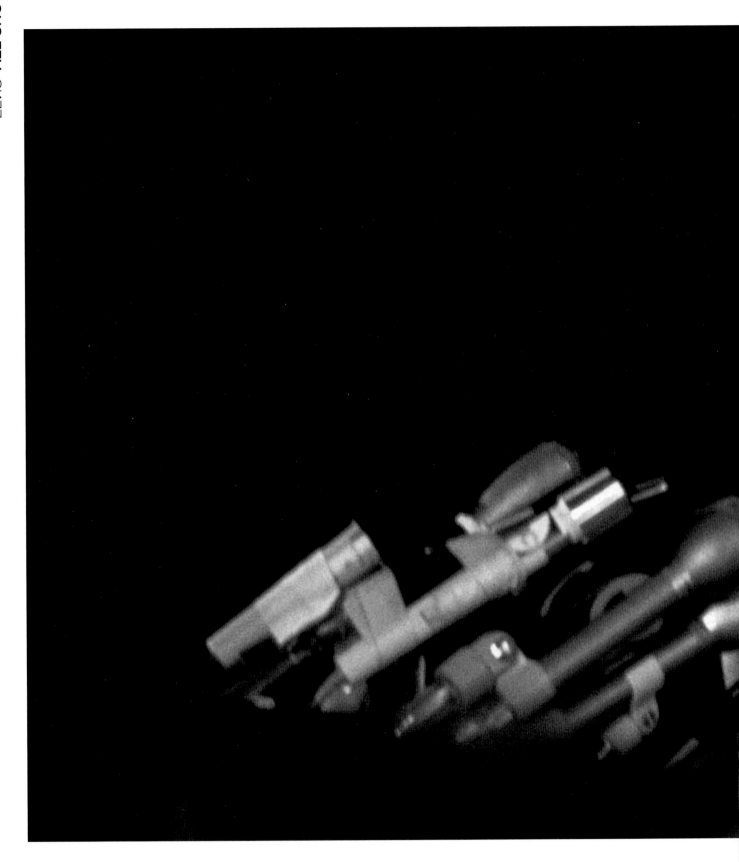

During the first number, his leg began to shake uncontrollably and a frisson of excitement ran through the female members of the audience. During the second number, they started to shout and, during the encore, they began to scream. The more he shook, the wilder they got. Sam Phillips, watching from the wings, was surprised and delighted by the crowd reaction. Even Slim Whitman mentioned Elvis during his set, saying that the boy was a hard act to follow. Back in the studios, they began searching for the next single. Elvis, still leaning towards ballads, suggested 'Blue Moon', a Rodgers and Hart song. Sam indulged him because, he said, "I didn't have the heart to stop him."

Elvis, now in charge, dropped the bridge and a verse and replaced them with a falsetto wordless melody, while Scotty, his guitar drenched in echo, did a clip-clop rhythm. The vocal, a masterpiece of timing and diction, was faultless. The result was an eerie, unworldly piece that Sam deemed too strange for a single, but it showed what Presley was capable of.

The next session produced six songs, including the next single, a Roy Brown R&B song called 'Good Rockin' Tonight', and the B-side, 'I Don't Care If The Sun Don't Shine', which showed the breadth of the material they were trying out. It had been a reject from Walt Disney's Cinderella, but had made it into the Dean Martin and Jerry Lewis film Scared Stiff. Elvis sung a snatch of it, Scotty and Bill jacked up the tempo and, almost before they realised, it was in the can. It features one of Elvis's most exuberant and humorous vocals. It's almost as if he couldn't believe he was singing it. When they weren't in the studio, Elvis, Scotty and Bill went out on the road doing an ever-widening circle of gigs, while Sam, a record man to the core, loaded up his car with copies of 'That's All Right' and hit the road, visiting distributors, radio stations and jukebox operators all over the south, spreading the word. Soon the record began to show up on the Billboard and

Cashbox regional charts and both magazines began to publish snippets and gig reviews about Elvis, calling him the "Hillbilly Cat".

During one of these trips, Sam called in at the Grand Ole Opry in Nashville and persuaded a reluctant management to put Elvis on the show, which went out live on air. The Opry was the home of country music and featured both the biggest stars and promising up-and-comers. It was a conservative institution that didn't take kindly to anybody who strayed too far from the pure country norm. But it was a gamble that Sam felt was worth taking.

The gamble didn't pay off. The crowd didn't warm to Elvis and all he got was polite applause. There was no question of a return booking. But they did get to meet some of their heroes, including Bill Monroe, the author of 'Blue Moon Of Kentucky'.

Rumour had it that Monroe had hated their version of his song and had promised to break Elvis's jaw if he ever met him, so there was some trepidation when they were introduced. However, Monroe told them how much he'd enjoyed their version, adding that he'd already cut a similar up-tempo version himself. Praise indeed. And Scotty got to meet his idol, Chet Atkins, who seemed disturbed that Elvis seemed to be wearing eye make-up. Elvis' physical appearance was causing some concern. His slicked-back greasy hair and long sideburns, coupled with his colourful, pimp-style clothes, seemed like an affront to crew-cutted, lumberjack-shirted American society.

And it was. Sam now turned his attention to the Louisiana Hayride, based in Shreveport. The Hayride was a similar operation to the Opry, smaller in reputation and scale but less purist and more open to new ideas. And they had been the first to feature Hank Williams and Slim Whitman. They had already expressed an interest in Elvis, but Sam had wanted to try the Opry first. When he called them they said yes immediately and Elvis was booked for the show two weeks later. There were two shows a night.

During the first, Elvis, Scotty and Bill were nervous and tentative. They got only polite applause. But on the second show, with a younger audience and after a half- time morale-boosting talk from Sam, Elvis exploded onto the stage and the crowd went wild. All the musicians watching agreed they'd never seen anything like it before...although, they further agreed, they thought his long, greasy duck-tail hair could have done with a wash.

" I'm not trying to be sexy. It's just my way of expressing myself when I move around. "

Elvis Presley

The Louisiana Hayride invited him to join the show on a regular basis and offered a year's contract, which Sam accepted.

'Good Rockin' Tonight', the next single, was released and moved onto the Billboard and Cashbox regional charts. For Elvis, Scotty and Bill there weren't enough hours in the day. They had all given up their jobs and were devoting every waking moment to music. If they weren't gigging, they were in the studio, searching for the next single. They found it in 'Milkcow Blues Boogie', a much-recorded song originally written by blues singer Kokomo Arnold. It was later a favourite of Bob Wills and the Texas Playboys, who performed it as a stately country song, but Elvis, Scotty and Bill came up with a relentless, piledriving version that left the listener breathless.

As Elvis's reputation grew he began to attract the attention of the managerial classes, showbusiness entrepreneurs and agents who could smell a dollar bill from a hundred miles away. Perhaps the most ruthless and calculating was Colonel Tom Parker, an ex-carnival hustler best known for 'Colonel Parker's Dancing Chickens', a major attraction on the carnival circuit. The chickens, caged and docile, suddenly became animated, jumping up and down when country music was played. They had no choice. The floor of their cage was a steel hot-plate which, when the Colonel turned it on, became a barbecue grill. They either danced or fried. But the carnival circuit was too small for the Colonel and he moved into country music, becoming Eddy Arnold's manager for a time before becoming Hank Snow's agent. He'd heard about Elvis and decided to take a look. He caught up with him at a Louisiana Hayride show. He was impressed, particularly by the screaming girls. He began to smell dollar bills. He made no move but did offer Elvis a down-the-bill spot on a Hank Snow show.

But during the next few days the Colonel went to see Steve Sholes, head of A&R at the country music section of RCA Records. He mentioned Elvis and told Sholes the kid was worth watching. Sholes showed enough interest to encourage the Colonel, who then went to a country music jamboree at the Ellis Auditorium in Memphis where Elvis was opening the show. It was here he met, for the first time, Sam Phillips, the man who, until then, had guided Elvis's career.

The pair took an instant dislike to one another and the encounter was acrimonious. The Colonel told Sam that Sun Records was too small an operation to handle an artist with as much potential as Elvis, adding that he should be signed to a record company with worldwide distribution, such as RCA. Sam knew he was right. Sun Records, with their limited distribution, could only take Elvis so far, but the Colonel's abrasive personality raised Phillips' hackles.

It was inevitable that the two such strong personalities would clash. Sam Phillips was a musical visionary and a deep thinker who saw music as having an intrinsic value. It was an end not a means. A creative force that, if harnessed properly, could change a society for the better.

The Colonel was a philistine to whom music was a means not an end, and artists were not creative entities. They were just more 'dancing chickens'. Sam's drive to create original music was matched by the Colonel's drive to make money. But Sam was also a shrewd businessman, who saw Presley's money-making potential. He kept his mouth shut and let the Colonel have his head. There was nothing he could do to stop him.

Back in Sun Studios, Elvis, Scotty and Bill, thanks to all the live work, were becoming confident and sure-footed. They came up with a string of classics: 'Mystery Train', 'Trying To Get To You', 'I Forgot To Remember To Forget' and 'Baby Let's Play House'. This last song – an arrogant, uptempo blues – was scheduled as the next single. When it was released it went straight in at Number 3 on the Cashbox country charts.

The Colonel, meanwhile, had secretly been to see Elvis's parents. He seduced them with talk of mass exposure, worldwide record deals, television appearances and movie stardom. They felt a little guilty about dumping Sam after all he had done for Elvis, but couldn't help but get excited about the Colonel's promises. The tide was beginning to turn. The Colonel, with the Presley parents onside, called Sam and offered to buy Elvis's contract. Sam, bowing to the inevitable, asked for $40,000 ($35,000, plus $5,000 he owed Elvis in back royalties).

Although Elvis was increasingly successful, Sam had considerable financial pressures, not least of which was a lawsuit with Duke Records who had stolen Junior Parker. Parker was one of Sam's artists who had written 'Mystery Train'. Manufacturing costs for records and royalties, a complex mass of time-lapsed payments, were spiralling, and he had other artists to worry about. Sam's new signing, Carl Perkins', first single, 'Blue Suede Shoes', was recorded and ready for release.

$40,000 doesn't sound much in this day and age, but at the time it was the largest deal ever paid for a single artist, including established stars. The Colonel balked at the deal but Sam stood firm, although a part of him wanted the deal to fall through. The Colonel put together a consortium that included RCA Records ($25,000 plus Elvis' back royalties was as high as they would go), Hill & Range music publishers (who came up with $5,000) and the Colonel himself (who put in $5,000 of his own money). On 21 November 1955, all the principals gathered in Sun Studios to sign the deal and Elvis Presley became an RCA Victor recording artist.

When it was over, Sam gave Elvis some parting advice. "Stand on your own," he said. "Don't let them tell you what to do. You know how to do it now, so do it your way."

In January, 1956, Elvis walked into RCA Studios in Nashville to cut his first sides for the RCA Victor label. Gone was the intimacy of Sun Studios, replaced by the cavernous formality of a studio that produced music in industrial proportions. They were booked in for three three-hour sessions over two days. Steve Sholes sat in the producer's chair. He had no plan other than to get as close to the Sun sound as possible. When Elvis asked him what he had in mind, he shrugged his shoulders and said, "Just do what you usually do."

Sholes may have wanted to duplicate the Sun sound but didn't know how to get it. They tried various ways to achieve the 'slapback' echo, but failed. That was Sam's secret. Sam's echo was a tape echo, but the closest the RCA team of engineers could get was to set up a microphone in a hallway and feed the effect back through the desk. It was a good, serviceable echo, but it wasn't the 'slapback' echo. They had no choice but to settle for it. Chet Atkins, RCA's man in Nashville and Scotty's hero, was hired to put a band together. The nucleus was Scotty and Bill, now augmented by a drummer, DJ Fontana, who had recently joined the live shows. Added to that were Atkins himself on rhythm guitar and newcomer Floyd Cramer on piano. Three backing singers, including Gordon Stoker from the Jordanaires, completed the line-up. While they were setting up, Scotty asked Chet Atkins what he had in mind. "Just do what you usually do," he replied.

The only person who knew what to do was Elvis who, while listening to any advice offered, confidently followed his own star, seemingly oblivious to the jangling nerves around him. He suggested 'I Got A Woman', the Ray Charles song that had become a staple of the live show.

Cramer clicked immediately and the song was in the can within the hour. The next song up was 'Heartbreak Hotel', a bleak blues that had also been in the act for a while. The song, written by

Mae Axton and Tommy Durden, wasn't an obvious choice for a single with lyrics that talked of broken-hearted lovers crying in the gloom, but Elvis had loved it when the writers had played it to him. "That's gonna be my first RCA single," he said. Cramer added a languid piano solo and, after a few takes, it was in the can.

It is almost impossible to overestimate the revolutionary nature of this track. Elvis's dramatic delivery drips with heartache, elevating what is essentially a blues into a gothic soundscape that seems to celebrate the tragic hopelessness of failed love. It was radically different to anything that had gone before. It didn't have the Sun Records sound, but it had a mordant grace that was unique. Atkins, a quiet, self-contained, country gentleman who probably had more experience of studio recording than any man alive, phoned his wife and told her to get down to the studio as soon as she could. "You'll never see anything like this again," he told her. "It's so damn exciting."

The next two sessions, one later that evening and one the following day, produced another three tracks: 'Money Honey', a cover of a Drifters song, and two ballads, 'I'm Counting On You' and 'I Was The One', the latter being selected as the prospective B-side for 'Heartbreak Hotel'. Sholes was worried because the five songs included two covers, two ballads and an unknown quantity. He wasn't sure about the potential of 'Heartbreak Hotel' as a single. Compared to the bright Sun sound it seemed dark and muddy. He was also worried about his failure to reproduce the 'slapback' echo. He was so desperate he even phoned Sam Phillips to ask him how to get it. "He's your boy now," Sam told him politely, " so you get it."

Sholes took the new songs and his doubts to RCA's headquarters in New York. His doubts were well-founded. The top brass hated it. "It didn't sound like the Sun records," they said, adding "it doesn't sound like anything." They expected better from the next sessions. Meanwhile, the Colonel had been lining up television shows. The first were six separate appearances, two weeks apart, on the Dorsey Brothers Show, based in New York. The Dorsey Brothers Show was well past its prime and their ratings were perilously low, but it was the first time Elvis had been exposed to a national audience. He exploded onto the stage, attacking the songs with boundless energy and his sheer delight at being on television was evident. Surprising everyone in his entourage, he didn't sing 'Heartbreak Hotel', preferring 'Shake, Rattle And Roll' which segued into 'Flip, Flop And Fly'. The sparse audience had never seen anything like it before and responded with both applause and embarrassed laughter.

> "Truth is like the sun. You can shut it out for a time, but it ain't goin' away."
>
> Elvis Presley

After the show, Elvis spent two days in the RCA studios in New York. The most significant song recorded at the sessions was a cover of Carl Perkins' 'Blue Suede Shoes'. Perkins was Sam Phillips' latest signing at Sun Records. Sam was using the RCA money well, his other signings including Jerry Lee Lewis, Johnny Cash and Roy Orbison. He also used some of the money to go into the hotel business with a business acquaintance. The first hotel was a success so they built another. Then another. In due course they had a chain of hotels. They called them Holiday Inns.

RCA realised that they had to have a new single to capitalise on the television exposure, so they shelved their doubts and released 'Heartbreak Hotel' as a single. On the back of the television exposure 'Heartbreak Hotel' went up the charts. RCA released the first album called 'Rock'n'Roll: Volume One', a mixture of newly recorded songs and unreleased Sun tracks. By the end of the shows, 'Heartbreak Hotel' was Number 1 in the national singles charts and the album Number 1 in its chart. And Hal Wallis, a Hollywood producer, had approached the Colonel, offering a screen test. The trade papers were calling Elvis "RCA's new singing sensation". The Colonel lined up a string of television shows including regular appearances on the Milton Berle Show and the Steve Allen Show, although the most prestigious, the Ed Sullivan Show, resisted.

Critical opinion was divided. Some thought Presley the most exciting performer ever to emerge from the American music scene and others thought him a joke. The latter criticised both his singing and his performance, calling it lewd. The press coined the epithet "Elvis the Pelvis" and used it ad nauseam. Elvis found it insulting. But controversy never harmed an artist's career prospects and the thousands of column inches devoted to the pros and cons of the Elvis phenomenon simply fuelled what was fast becoming a national debate. Juvenile delinquency was considered a nationwide

problem and Elvis was seen as a contributory factor in its growth, especially as most of the teenage tearaways were now sporting Elvis Presley hairstyles and sideburns.

The next television appearance was the Milton Berle Show, staged on the deck of the aircraft carrier USS Hancock, berthed in San Diego harbour. The show was memorable because Elvis delivers one of the great rock'n'roll performances of all time. Bill Black, caught up in the moment, rides his double-bass like a horse, slapping both sides of it, and the audience, made up of sailors and their girlfriends, go wild. The performance is crowned by an unforeseen moment of high comedy when the wake of a passing ship rocks the Hancock, throwing all the TV cameras out of kilter, cutting the head off Elvis and the band.
After the show, the Colonel threatened Bill Black with the sack for the bass-slapping incident, because it took the attention away from Elvis. Bill, chastened, never did it again. At least when the Colonel was around.
'Heartbreak Hotel' stayed at Number 1 for eight weeks, selling two million copies and earning Elvis his first gold disc. Life had become a frenetic round of gigs, television appearances and studio work, and the search was on for a follow-up single. They found it on 14 April at RCA Studios in Nashville, a ballad called, 'I Want You, I Need You, I Love You'. There were 300,000 advance orders, the largest in RCA's history.

The next Milton Berle Show proved to be a quantum leap in the Presley legend. Elvis sang a yet-to-be-recorded song called 'Hound Dog', a Jerry Leiber/ Mike Stoller blues shouter that had been a minor hit for Big Mama Thornton. For the first time Elvis ditched the guitar and, with freshly-dyed black hair, delivered a performance that eclipsed everything that had gone before.

His movements were less frantic and more calculated, now tailored to highlight the dynamics of the song. He punctuated DJ's machine-gun rolls with a blur of leg snaps that drew delighted applause from the audience. Halfway through the song the band half-timed the tempo, and Elvis went up a gear. The mood changed. He appeared out of control, totally immersed in the rhythm, and the leg snaps, now slower, became overtly sexual. The audience was now in a frenzy, just where Elvis wanted them. He lowered his head, trying, unsuccessfully, to hide a smile. This was pure, unfettered genius.

Elvis frightened the life out of both the TV networks and the critics. The next day's press branded him "vulgar" and "obscene" and called for him to be banned.

The Daughters Of The American Revolution, a right wing, Bible- punching pressure group, released a statement saying they feared the effect he may be having on the nation's young people, and radio stations throughout the country dropped him from their playlists. The TV networks were caught on the horns of a dilemma. They had to show him because their ratings soared every time they did, but they were terrified of showing anything that would upset middle America. They offered a compromise. They would continue to feature him on their programmes but they would only show him from the waist up.

Elvis was hurt and bemused, but the Colonel, who believed that any publicity was good publicity, was ecstatic. RCA, for their part, couldn't press records fast enough to meet the demand. Elvis arrived in Hollywood to make his first film, a Western originally entitled The Reno Brothers starring Richard Egan and Debra Paget. To cash in on Presley's popularity, four songs were added and the film re-titled Love Me Tender. It was released to mixed reviews, but at every theatre it played there were queues around the block. The film recouped its production costs in three days and the single of the title song generated, for the first time in music-industry history, over one million advance orders.

The demand for new material was insatiable and Elvis was constantly in the studio. The band were now augmented by the Jordanaires, a well-known gospel quartet. Gospel quartets were ubiquitous in the Southern states and during his teenage years Elvis had auditioned, unsuccessfully, for several. Gospel was Elvis's first love so it was a natural progression for him to turn to the Jordanaires when vocal backings were needed, and their sublime arrangements added a vital ingredient to the Presley sound. At a session in RCA studios in New York he finally recorded 'Hound Dog'.

Chet Atkins was no longer present to covertly supervise the sessions because it was obvious that Elvis knew exactly what he wanted. The 'Hound Dog' session was the perfect example. They recorded take after take of the song. Steve Sholes thought they had it in the first few takes but Elvis politely sidelined him and carried on.

Finally after thirty-one takes Elvis pronounced himself satisfied. He then listened to playbacks of all the takes, sitting cross- legged in front of the speakers. After take twenty-eight, he stood up, smiled and, to everyone's relief, said, "That's the one." When 'Hound Dog' was in the can, they cut two more songs: 'Don't Be Cruel', an Otis Blackwell song, and 'Any Way You Want Me', probably the most dramatic ballad Elvis ever recorded.

'Don't Be Cruel' and 'Hound Dog' were released as a double A-sided single, and they charted separately, 'Don't Be Cruel' reaching Number 1 and 'Hound Dog' reaching Number 2. Not even the mighty Ed Sullivan could ignore this and Elvis was booked for America's most important TV show. Shot from just the waist up, Elvis did a mesmerising 'Don't Be Cruel'.

The next movie was Loving You, with a plot loosely-based on Elvis' rise to fame. It featured some great songs including the iconic 'Teddy Bear', which was released as a single, and an unforgettable 'Mean Woman Blues', with Elvis at his incendiary best. 'Teddy Bear' went straight to Number 1, selling over a million copies and earning him another gold disc. This established a pattern. Each new single was eagerly awaited by an audience with a ravenous hunger for more Elvis music, and he couldn't make records fast enough to cope with the demand. Each new single had huge advance orders. Each new single sold a million plus copies, earning him another gold disc. This was supply and demand at its most acute. And the reason was simple. Elvis was making perfect records. The music was highly original, musically groundbreaking, and each was totally different from what had gone before. Elvis used a different vocal approach to every song, infusing the track with his personality. Scotty Moore's guitar solos matched Elvis for originality, creating great slabs of abstract guitar that never went where you thought they were going to. It was impossible for the records not to sell a million copies.

The next film was Jailhouse Rock. The title track alone was worth the price of admission. Another Leiber and Stoller song, it flew to Number 1 in the American charts when released as a single. In Great Britain it was the first single to go straight in at Number 1. It seemed that nothing could stop him. Then came the bombshell. He was drafted into the US Army.

If the Colonel had pulled some strings, he could have got out of it. But Elvis wanted to serve his country. And, what was more, he wanted no favours. He wanted to serve his country as a regular GI. There would be no concerts entertaining the troops and no recording during his two years' service. There would be a complete cessation of his musical career.

The Colonel had no choice but to agree. He began to see the publicity value in Elvis doing his patriotic duty. The Colonel saw it as a way to steer his charge away from the rebellious image. This could be the first step in turning him into a wholesome family entertainer.

Elvis was due to start filming on his new movie King Creole. If he were drafted into the army immediately the film would have to be cancelled and hundreds of people would lose their jobs, so he was granted a deferment and the movie went ahead.

King Creole was based on the Harold Robbins best-seller A Stone For Danny Fisher. Elvis played a night-club singer caught up in the New Orleans underworld. The film was given extra weight by the presence of Walter Matthau as a ruthless mobster. Elvis acquitted himself well in a film that was a highly convincing drama, interspersed with classic rock performances including a spine-tingling delivery of 'Trouble'. The title song was released as a single and immediately qualified for a gold disc.

Elvis also used the deferment to record a stock of singles to be released during his period of service. These included 'A Big Hunk O'Love', 'A Fool Such As I', and 'I Got Stung'. That done, he reported to the Memphis recruitment office on 24 March 1958 and became Private Presley. In a blaze of publicity, which pleased the army as much as it did the Colonel, he was photographed as a military barber shaved the sideburns off and stripped the iconic hairstyle down to stubble. In retrospect, it could be seen as the moment that symbolised the end of the dangerous rebel and the start of the wholesome family entertainer.

After basic training he was posted to Germany as part of the 2nd Medium Tank Battalion of the Armoured Division, where he spent the rest of his service. Before leaving America he did one final press conference, which was released as a spoken-word EP. It immediately sold over a million copies. Once in Germany, he was allowed to live off-base. He rented a house and shipped his entourage over from America.

He only left the house when duty called. The house became a part of Germany that was forever America. During Elvis's absence, the Colonel worked tirelessly to keep him in the public mind, helped by the staggered release of the stock of singles. They were all million-sellers. But the Colonel had never understood the value of Elvis's music, or its revolutionary nature. It was just a means to an end, another piece of the jigsaw. He wanted Elvis to be a movie star, making films the whole family could go and see. The teenage market was a niche market, albeit a huge one, but soon they would grow up and settle down. He wanted an Elvis that would appeal to everybody, and that meant an end to the rebel image. It could only be achieved by knocking the rough edges off Elvis and presenting him as wholesome and inoffensive. For Elvis, it meant artistic death. Elvis was demobbed in March 1960.

His homecoming was that of a hero. The Colonel, his grand strategy now in place, had lined up a welcome home TV special hosted by Frank Sinatra. Almost straight afterwards he was due to start shooting his new film, GI Blues. But first he spent a day in RCA's studios in Nashville. The band contained a few familiar faces. Scotty Moore was on guitar, DJ Fontana was one of the drummers used, Floyd Cramer played piano and the Jordanaires provided the backing vocals. Elvis recorded six songs, including his first post-army single, 'Stuck On You'. It was a rock'n'roll song with a shuffle beat, and Elvis showed he had lost none of the magic. It was a promising start.

The TV special was a huge success, garnering 65% of the viewing audience. The broadcasting company were relieved because Elvis's fee was a staggering $125,000.

The Colonel was taking no prisoners. On 3 April 1960 Elvis spent the day in RCA's studio in Nashville recording his first post-army album, 'Elvis Is Back', with the same band as the 'Stuck On You' sessions. In ten-and-a-half hours, they recorded an astonishing 12 songs, including his next two singles, 'It's Now Or Never' and 'Are You Lonesome Tonight', which

didn't appear on the album. 'Elvis Is Back' featured some astonishing performances. 'Fever', the Peggy Lee hit, was Elvis at his most sensual and 'Such A Night' bubbled with suggestiveness. RCA, delighted, rushed the album out.

Before Elvis started shooting GI Blues, he first had to record the soundtrack, but this was dogged with problems. It started with an acrimonious row over the selection of songs that would have negative repercussions on Elvis's career. Leiber and Stoller were invited to submit some songs, a logical request since they had been Elvis's principal writers before he went into the army. They had written, among many

others, 'Hound Dog', 'Jailhouse Rock' and 'King Creole'. They were already disenchanted with the Colonel, whom they considered an ignorant man with no artistic vision, but they nevertheless offered a batch of new songs. They soon found themselves embroiled in a protracted dispute with the Colonel who insisted that, before their songs would be considered for the film, they would have to sign the copyright over to the Presley estate.

Then Jerry Leiber, with the best of intentions, suggested to the publishing company that Elvis should star in a film version of Walk On The Wild Side, directed by Elia Kazan. When the Colonel heard about this he was furious. Going behind his back to discuss Presley business with a third party was, in the Colonel's eyes, the last straw and he swore that Leiber and Stoller would never write for Elvis again.

This was fine with Leiber and Stoller, whose songs were much in demand across the industry. But the Colonel had deprived Elvis of a goldmine of songs. GI Blues was not a great film, nor was it intended to be. It was just a piece of froth, made quickly to cash in on Elvis's military service. But Leiber and Stoller would at least have lent some weight to the proceedings. However, thanks to legions of Elvis-starved fans, it was a box-office hit.

What came next was astounding. 'It's Now Or Never' was released as a single. It was an anglicised remake of 'O Sole Mio', the old Neapolitan love song, which Elvis sang in a suitably operatic voice. It sold five million copies in America alone and a million in Britain. Similar sales figures came in from all over the world, making 'It's Now Or Never' the second most successful song in recording history after Bing Crosby's 'White Christmas'. But instead of capitalising on this, the Colonel sent Elvis off to Hollywood to continue his movie career.

The next two films, Flaming Star, a violent Western, and Wild In The Country a rather thoughtful film about a budding writer, showed that Presley could act, but his fourth film, Blue Hawaii, a huge box-office success, started the downward spiral. The flimsy plot featured Elvis as a likeable guy singing forgettable songs in beautiful locations. This set the template for the rest of his movie career. For the next seven years he starred in films that would not have taxed the intellect of a five year-old child. He hated doing them, but that's what the Colonel wanted. Unchallenging family entertainment.

His recording output, deprived of songs by the best writers who refused to sign their copyrights away, also declined. In the previous decade, a Presley release was a much-awaited cultural event, but now Elvis records came and went seemingly unnoticed. The law of diminishing returns meant that his fan-base dwindled and he was written off by a generation of critics. The Beatles conquered the world and changed the face of popular music. Why listen to Elvis when you could listen to The Beatles?

There was a mini-renaissance in 1967 when Elvis decided to record 'Guitar Man', a self-penned hit for sublime country guitarist Jerry Reed. It was a great rocking song, but they couldn't nail it down in the studio because nobody could play the highly individual guitar part. So they invited Reed to join the session. He did and everything clicked into place. It was the best piece of work Elvis had produced for years. But then the Colonel nearly blew the whole thing by insisting that Reed sign over the copyright of the song. Reed refused and threatened to walk out. Elvis intervened and the Colonel, for the first time in his life, backed off. They celebrated by recording another of Reed's numbers, 'Big Boss Man'. Both songs burned brightly for a while, then Elvis went back on the treadmill.

When, in 1968, NBC Television announced that Elvis was scheduled to record a live Comeback Special, the heart of every Elvis fan in the world beat a little faster. The additional information that Scotty Moore and DJ Fontana were involved seemed too good to be true.

The show had started out as a Christmas show that Colonel Parker had negotiated with NBC. NBC hired Steve Binder as producer. Binder didn't much like Elvis but, as things progressed, he realised what impact the show might have. He determined to show the real Elvis – Elvis, the artist. He came up with the idea of opening the show with a jam session. Surrounded by musicians he was familiar with, Elvis would sing his rock'n'roll songs, interspersed with banter about the old days.

He floated the idea to Colonel Parker, who hated it. The Colonel was still thinking of Christmas trees and chestnuts roasting on an open fire. But Elvis liked the idea. The Colonel reluctantly agreed, as long as the show then returned to its Christmas format. But the tide had turned, mainly due to Elvis, who wanted the show to be a serious attempt at restoring his musical credibility.

Gradually all references to Christmas were stripped away until only the final song remained to be decided. The Colonel was implacable. It was going to be a Christmas song, and that was that.

Steve Binder, now totally committed, thought the only way around it was to deal with Elvis directly. But what should the final song be? He approached Earl Brown, the show's vocal arranger, and asked him to write a song that would sum up Elvis's life. Brown spent the night writing and, by the morning, had come up with a song called, 'If I Can Dream'. Binder loved it and, behind the Colonel's back, got Brown to sing the song to Elvis. The song is a turgid power-ballad with trite, aspirational lyrics, but Elvis loved it. Sam Philips would have laughed it out of the studio. But once Elvis was convinced, the Colonel had to give way. The show was complete. Scotty Moore and DJ Fontana flew in and rehearsals began. Everybody concerned agreed that the resulting music was wonderful.

On the day the show was recorded, Elvis, consumed by nerves, tried to back out of the jam-session section. He wasn't worried about the musical side of things but, without a script, he was afraid the ad-libs might dry up. But Binder, in no uncertain terms, put his foot down. It was too late to back out. Prompt sheets were given to the musicians, suggesting stories to tell and ad-libs that would be jumping-off points. The set for the session was called the 'boxing ring' because the podium was of a similar size. The musicians would sit in a circle. They would be surrounded by a small crowd of about two hundred hand-picked people. The Colonel made sure that all the prettiest girls would be closest to the front.

Elvis looked magnificent. Looking fit and tanned, his raven-black hair glinting in the studio lights, he was dressed in a black leather outfit designed by NBC's wardrobe department. Elvis played his blonde Gibson J-200 acoustic. Scotty sat to his immediate left playing his Gibson electric and DJ sat in front

of him, playing on an empty guitar case. Charlie Hodge played acoustic and Alan Fortas, one of Elvis's cronies who wasn't even a musician, played tambourine. Lance Legault, Elvis's film double, sat behind him on the podium, also playing tambourine. They kicked off with 'That's All Right'. It sounded a little ragged but the old magic was still there. They followed it with 'Heartbreak Hotel'. Elvis messed the words up and the band lost their way, but he laughed it off.

The third song was a bluesy version of 'Love Me', during which Elvis seemed to relax. Then he made a huge mistake. He changed guitars with Scotty. A look of horror flashed across Scotty's face. Now Elvis was playing the rhythm on an electric guitar, completely obliterating Scotty on acoustic. Without Scotty's revolutionary guitar, the music became one-dimensional. Elvis carried the set by sheer force of personality, but something had been lost. As the set progressed, it became apparent that he was trying too hard. Nobody could judge the dynamics of a song better than Elvis. He knew instinctively when to lay back and when to open the throttle. But here, he delivered the vocals in a raucous shout, devoid of subtlety. Still, it was better than anybody had seen since before his army service.

When the jam session was over, the next segment remained on the boxing ring. The band left and now Elvis was alone, backed by an off-screen orchestra. He sang 'Memories', a plodding ballad beloved of a million cabaret crooners, and the mood of expectation was instantly dissipated. The show rallied briefly when he sang 'Guitar Man', but the presentation, complete with go-go dancers, owed more to his cinema career than live performance. 'If I Can Dream' closed the show. In dramatic lighting, Elvis sang the song as if it was the last he would ever sing. He threw everything into it with a desperate intensity that gave the song an emotional punch it otherwise lacked. When the show was over, everybody involved was euphoric. It had been an unqualified success. Even the Colonel was happy.

Elvis considered it a watershed in his life. A rebirth. A new dawn. He told the Colonel he was finished with Hollywood and he wanted to tour again. "I never want to do another film I don't like," he said, "and I never want to sing another song I don't like, ever again." When the show was aired the following December it was regarded, by critics and audiences alike, as an unqualified success. After nearly a decade in the artistic wilderness, Elvis was back.

It may have been a watershed for Elvis, but changing course wasn't that easy. He still had three more film commitments to honour but this would give the reluctant Colonel some time to organise the live gigs. This was the pivotal moment. Like the great blues singer Robert Johnson before him, he was standing at a crossroads. Following the right road could lead him to a return to artistic rebirth, but a wrong turning could consign him to cabaret irrelevance. It started promisingly with a change of tack on the recording front. For years he had been recording in RCA's studios around the country, but now a couple of close friends suggested he try an independent studio. They suggested American Studios in Memphis, run by Chips Moman, a friend of theirs. American was a hot studio and Chips, a hands-on producer, had rejuvenated the ailing careers of several artists, including Wilson Pickett and Dusty Springfield. Elvis agreed. He started thinking about songs. He was after a new direction, something different.

Since he had come out of the army, song selection had been placed in the hands of Freddy Bienstock, whose choice of material depended more on whether the songwriter was prepared to hand over copyright to Elvis Presley Enterprises than the quality of the song. Freddy Bienstock was an administrator working for Elvis's publishing company, Hill & Range. Since the beginning of the RCA deal Bienstock's job was to provide Elvis with a selection of material. But this time Elvis would pick the songs. Neither Chips nor the studio band were particularly impressed by the prospect of

working with Elvis. As far as they were concerned, he was a has- been, a musical irrelevance. But as soon they started running through the songs, his commitment and work-rate ensured that the sessions soon caught fire. By the time the sessions were over, they had the next two singles in the can. 'In The Ghetto' and 'Suspicious Minds', both a departure from the 'old' Elvis. Things were looking good. Then the Colonel came up with the gig sheet.

The obvious choice, hinted at by Elvis in interviews, was a worldwide tour. Elvis had never performed outside America and there was a global audience hungry for their first sight of Presley in the flesh. Instead the Colonel had booked him a month-long residency at the International Hotel in Las Vegas. The cabaret circuit. An artistic graveyard. Instead of an audience of genuine Elvis fans he would be providing entertainment for gamblers, looking for something to do after a hard day on the fruit machines. The Colonel had blown it.

Several theories have been advanced seeking to explain the Colonel's reluctance to tour Elvis in Europe, but recent research has come up with an interesting hypothesis. The Colonel was Dutch by birth and emigrated to America in his twenties. Just before he left Holland, there was a murder in his home town. To this day the murder remains unsolved. Could it be that the Colonel was afraid to return to European jurisdiction? It's just a theory. Whatever the reason, Elvis would never tour outside America.

Elvis had played Las Vegas once before, during the rock'n'roll years. It had been a disaster and he had sworn never to play there again, but now he agreed. Maybe he just wanted to get on a stage again and it didn't matter where the stage happened to be. But the Colonel's limited vision had ensured that the golden moment when Elvis could have become culturally relevant again had passed. The chance was missed.

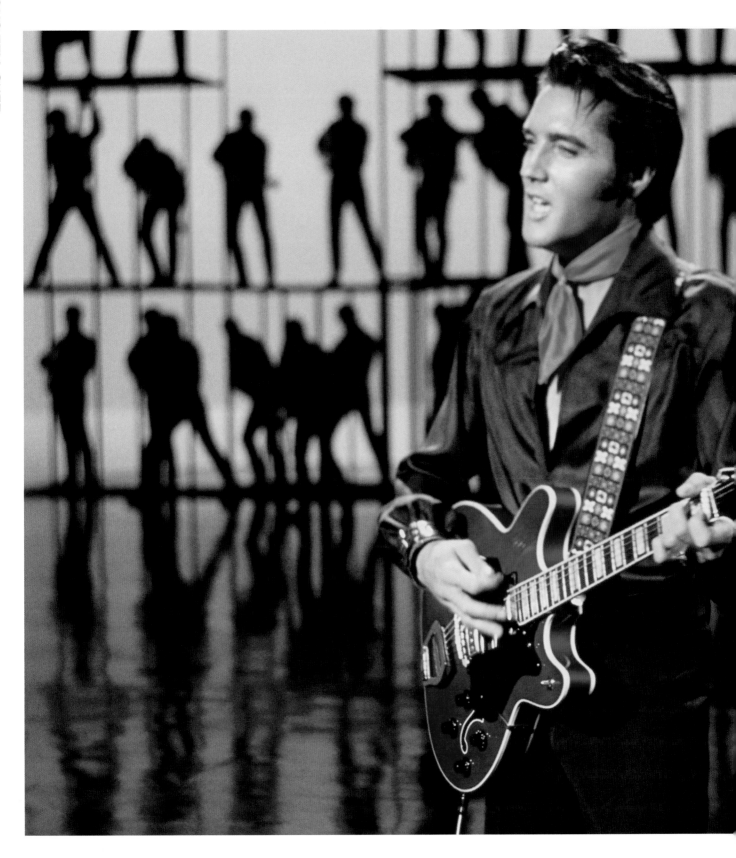

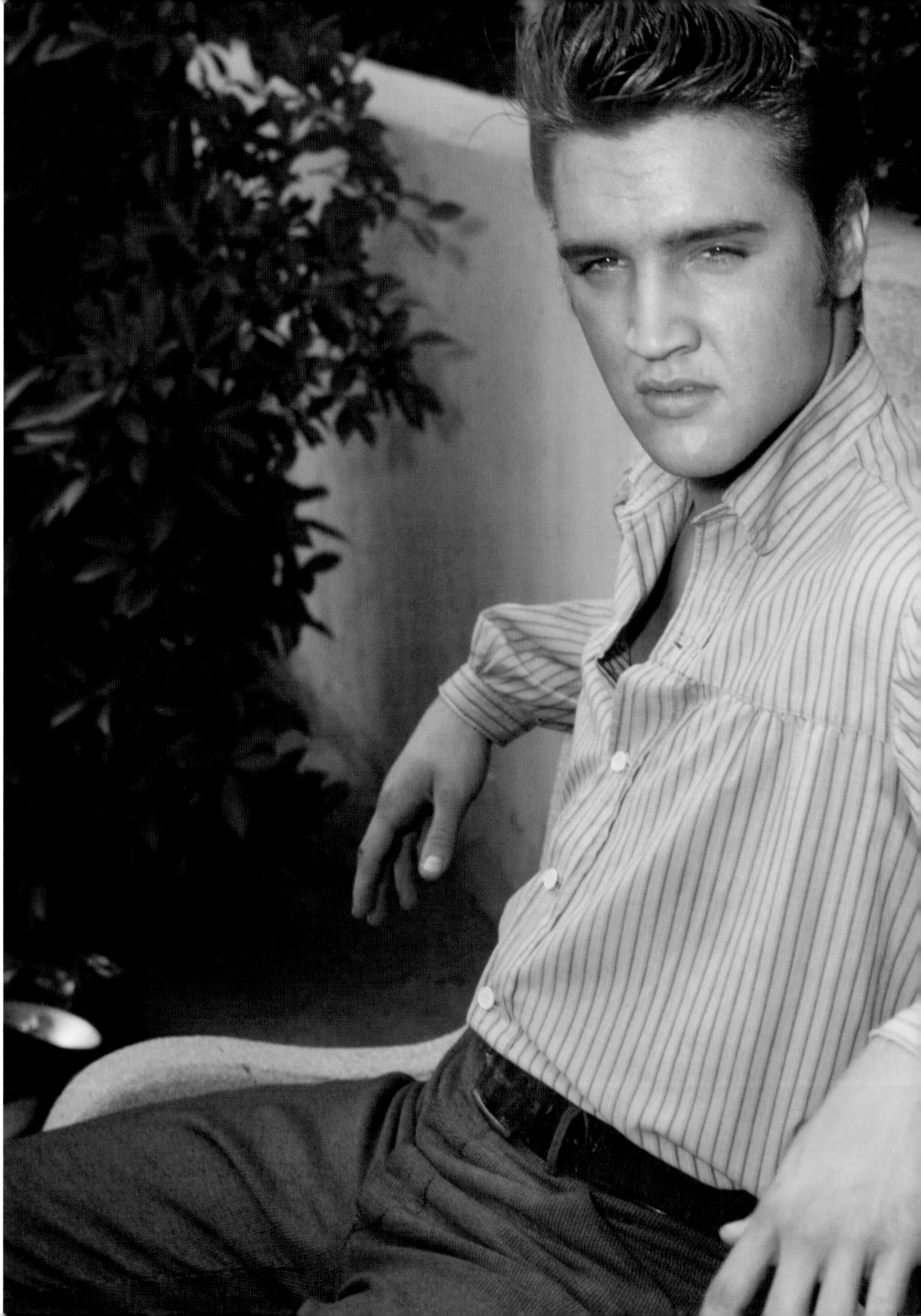

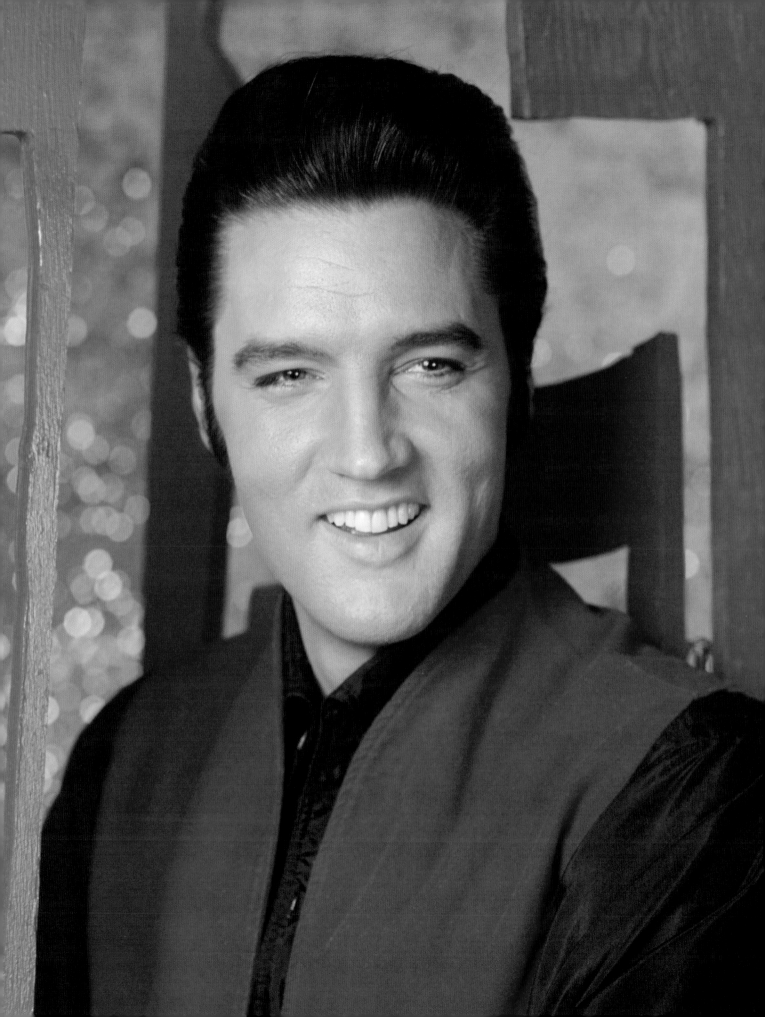

He was back on the treadmill. But Elvis threw himself into live work with relish. He phoned James Burton, a groundbreaking guitarist who had been the redeeming factor of Ricky Nelson's records, and asked him to put a band together for the Las Vegas gigs. He tried to book the Jordanaires for vocal backing, but they were now big stars, and found it impossible to fit the Presley shows in.

So he hired the Imperials, who he'd worked with on the 'How Great Thou Art' album and the Sweet Inspirations, who been Aretha Franklin's vocal back-ups. He added an orchestra partly because it would have been expected by the Las Vegas audience. It was not an artistic decision. The set list was mostly made up of his back catalogue, with a few nods to contemporary music including the Beatles songs 'Yesterday' and 'Hey Jude'. Another concession to the Las Vegas audience? The Colonel finally reminded him just before he went on stage to avoid doing anything "off-colour" because "there might be children out there."

The opening night was a huge success. The audience of 2,000 was liberally sprinkled with celebrities. Even Cary Grant was spotted dancing on a table. Elvis, releasing almost a decade of pent-up inaction, hurled himself into the performance, leaving the audience, and himself, drained and breathless. And it was the same night after night.

His entourage worried that he might collapse from nervous exhaustion, but Elvis, seemingly, had limitless reserves of energy. He had a point to prove and he was going to damn well prove it. He ended the month in a state of bliss. The hit of the show was a six-minute version of 'Suspicious Minds'. It was immediately released as a single and moved quickly to Number 1 in the charts.

The Press were universally impressed. As far as they were concerned, Elvis was back, firing on all cylinders. So favourable were the reviews that the Colonel started booking a nationwide tour. And when that was over, Elvis was scheduled to return for another month in Las Vegas. This set the pattern for the rest of his life. Two months a year in Las Vegas and yearly comprehensive tours of the United States. Gone were the infantile movies. There were still films but now they were documentaries showing the life of a musician on the road, Elvis – That's The Way It Is and Elvis On Tour.

The singles kept on coming. The magisterial 'In The Ghetto' was followed by the mawkish 'Don't Cry Daddy'. The quality didn't seem to matter. They both went to Number 1 in the charts, selling a million copies along the way.

In 1973, the Colonel pulled off a big one. A 90-minute TV special from Honolulu called Aloha From Hawaii. This was beamed, via satellite, around the world, to the largest audience for any single TV event.

But by now the cracks were beginning to show. The malign influence of Las Vegas was becoming dominant. The rock'n'roll content of the set was diminishing and the big, schmaltzy cabaret numbers were taking precedence. Songs like 'Hound Dog', once epic centrepieces of his performance, were now relegated to a perfunctory two verses in the middle of a medley. The genuine emotional pain of 'Heartbreak Hotel' had disappeared, giving way to the ersatz patriotism of 'American Trilogy'. Ominously, too, Elvis was putting on weight.

And things just got worse. His health deteriorated and he began to rely more and more on drugs prescribed by his personal physician. His eating binges became legendary and he became obese. He became bored with performing and put most of what energy he had left into planning a film about karate. His choice of songs was now governed by the Las Vegas ethic, sinking to its nadir when he began performing the Frank Sinatra hit 'My Way' which had become a valedictory anthem for third-rate cabaret crooners. However, surrounded by his sycophantic entourage, there was no-one to question his actions, and the Colonel, who couldn't tell a good song from a dancing chicken, was too busy counting the money.

On 21 June 1977 he played what was to be his last gig at the Rushmore Civic Centre in Rapid City. It was a near disaster. Elvis, now grossly overweight, stumbled around the stage, seemingly in a state of near-collapse. Aides waited in the wings, ready to run on and catch him should he fall. The low point came when he introduced 'Are You Lonesome Tonight'. Obviously befuddled, he lost the thread and embarked on a stream-of-consciousness introduction, almost as if talking to himself, that ends in an incoherent mumble. It is embarrassing and immeasurably sad.

He died on the morning of 16 August 1977, the day he was scheduled to start another tour. The Colonel, when asked about his reaction to Elvis's death said, "It's just like when he went in the army," and carried on promoting his now posthumous star.

But Elvis had left the building. His career had moved back and forth between the sublime and the ridiculous. Sometimes he was an admired trailblazer, taking music into uncharted territory, and sometimes he was a fat has-been, no more than the Colonel's dancing chicken. But in his prime he was simply peerless. It is hard not to come to the conclusion that his army service mortally injured the artist in him.

Before the army he had been a force of nature, uninhibited and instinctive, but his two-year sabbatical gave him time to think and he returned to the world wearing a cloak of self- consciousness. It smothered his matchless talent and he could never, except for the occasional brief, shining moment, recapture the glory days. Ironically, he ended his life almost as an Elvis impersonator.

But the ignominious tragedy of his final years should not overshadow the achievement of his glory days. He was the most successful artist of the 20th Century. He created seismic shifts in popular music that created tremors that still rumble to this day. He was the template on which thousands of artists based their careers, a benchmark against which they could judge their own efforts. Today, he is simply remembered as The King. That is the mother of all understatements.

" I don't know anything about music. In my line you don't have to. "

Elvis Presley

Interview with DJ Fontana

I met Scotty, Bill and Elvis at the Louisiana hayride down in Shreveport, Louisiana. I had heard their records, they wer playing rock in that one area and one of the managers called me there one day and said "I want you to listen to this record". So I went to his office and they played it and I said How many guys they got playing in this band?" and they said" Just 3 guys" and it sounded like 5 or 6 people with the echo and everything and I said "Boy that's awfully good."

So anyway, they come in and Scotty said "would you like to work with those tonight?" and I said "Yeah, well that's why I'm here" so I said "Let's go back into the dressing room and kind of talk about it". So Elvis got his guitar and Scotty and Bill and they just played a little bit and I said "Yeah, we can do that then". So we did it that night and he'd come back in a few weeks later and we did it again. Two or three weeks and he'd come back in and out. So that's how it basically got started. Just by accident I happened to be there.

Q. What were your first impressions of Elvis as a musician, what did you make of him?

Well, his voice was so unusual for that time period and his clothes were unusual – his dress with the peg pants and all that stuff and stripes down his pants leg. And he was a good looking kid, a good looking guy and I said "Hey this guy might do ok – who knows?" he had that certain charisma about him that there was no way for him to miss, no way.

Q. What was the music scene like then? Was Elvis ahead of his time?

Yeah, well I think he was a little bit ahead of his time. We were all still listening to the big bands – Woody Herman, Stan Kenton, those kinds of guys. The Dorsey Brothers – that's all we had basically on radio. They had a couple of blues stations but they didn't get out very far – 5,000 miles and stuff like that and so we were really into the big band listening.

> " A live concert to me is exciting because of all the electricity that is generated in the crowd and on stage. It's my favorite part of the business, live concerts. "

Elvis Presley

Q. What kind of drummer are you yourself? Where did you get a lot of your influences?

From the big bands, listening to those guys play and watching them, if they'd come in town. Sometimes every now and again there would be a big orchestra come through town on a one nighter. And we'd all go out and see them play and you learn a little bit from each one of the guys.

Q. How did it feel going from behind the curtain to in front of the curtain?

Oh it was different yeah it was just a farce I think. Basically the country acts and the country programmes wasn't really for me with drums at all. So they weren't sure how the people would take us so they'd say "Well you stand back there and play" and I'd say "Well that's alright with me" you get paid the same money you know. And every couple of weeks they'd say "Well, just bring a snare drum out and bring a cymbal out" and by the time we'd got through with Elvis they had the whole set out he said "Just bring them all out".That's what he wanted and that's what Elvis wanted so I guess maybe they kind of figured they'd better go along with his wishes I guess cos he was drawing a lot of people in there by then.

Q. So obviously what you were used to was different from what Elvis was playing? What kind of music was being played, where was the influence coming from?

I think they'd come from a lot of black groups being from a Memphis area and he'd listened to a lot of black radio programmes. Scotty was a kind of a blues, jazz player he wanted to be and Bill was just an all-round bass player, that's not country not pop just, the feel of that's what he did, he had good feeling to his bass playing.

Q. What kind of drums were you using? What kind of sound were you trying to achieve?

Well I had Gretsch drums and so that's all I really knew, what they sounded like and I used them on all the early records – we did a lot here in RCAB here, did a lot in California - I'd ship them on a plane. And back then you could do that without them getting hurt, they really took care of them where nowadays they throw them around so bad I wouldn't dare send anything in that luggage like that. But they really took care of equipment, all the equipment.

Q. Was there anything different about the way you played drums on the music like time signatures or was it just straight hit?

No straight hit basically - you just play what you want to play basically. All the stuff we did early was hit arrangements. He'd play an acetate right here in the middle of the floor and he'd say "Yeah well we'll keep that one" and they he'd throw another one on a pile over there, he didn't like that. And he'd say "Well let's see what we can do with this one" and we'd pick out something and he'd say "Just play it and if it doesn't feel right we'll get another feel". It was up to him basically. Usually he was right so I'd say "Well you want me to play this?" "No don't play this play something else". So you just kind of listened to what he wanted, that's what we did.

Q. Tell me a bit about Heartbreak Hotel and Jailhouse Rock, Teddy Bear …

Heartbreak was done not too far from here actually and it was a kind of an old ex-church, cathedral like – it was a small place but that was what they used it as at one time. And there wasn't a so-called echo chambers like they have even in this studio and they ran some mike cords and mikes down the hallway for echo on the record, that's how the sound of that, they wanted to get the old Sun sound on the Heartbreak Hotel but it just wasn't the same. It never was the same. But they tried.

Q. Did you do any recordings in here? Can you tell us more about where we are right now?

We're in RCAB – we probably did hundreds of them right here in this studio – Stuck on You, some I can't remember all of them now – you got a list? There was just hundreds of them.

Q. And what did you make of Elvis as a person and a musician and an actor?

I thought he was good – he was a good musician, he knew in his mind what he wanted to hear and sometimes he'd have a hard time explaining it to you because he wasn't the best musician – none of us were good musicians but we knew kind of what his thinking was so we basically went along with him and somehow or other it worked, it really worked well.

Q. Do you think this Elvis phenomenon happened overnight or did it evolve gradually?

No it took a little while. But we worked some real some dives you might say and we worked some high school gyms, some little Friday night football stadiums so we did a lot of that for I guess a year and a half or so. It didn't really bust right open until we went up to do the Dorsey Shows.

And then people saw him and he kept getting bigger and bigger and bigger and then we did the Sinatra show and we did this show and that show, all the main television programmes of that time period, we did them all.

Q. What was life on the road like when you were travelling around?

Well, we had one car, me, Scotty and Bill and Elvis had all our instruments in that one car. Sometimes he'd bring Jean Smith with him who was his cousin, sometimes Billy, another cousin and other times Red West so it was a car full of people and instruments but somehow or other we all got in there and we had

a great time. Well you couldn't do much just sit there and talk. You couldn't move around much cos it was just too crowded, too many people.

Q. Tell us about your fellow musicians, Scotty and Bill – tell us a bit about what they're like as musicians to work with?

They're easy to work with, all of the guys were easy to work with. They knew what he wanted cos they knew him a little while before I did so we all just kind of played it basically by ear. Scotty had to play rhythm and lead at the same time and that made it hard for him. So when I joined the band he said "I'm glad you got here cos, boy, I always have to do it all". You know which, that's what he did. He said "Now I can count, you know play more lead or whatever without losing the whole bottom end of it" and Bill's slapping his bass. We had a great sound I thought.

Q. And Scotty as a manager?

He was a road manager for a while and the reason for that I think is that you could go up and say "Elvis we want to do this benefit". "OK I'll do it". He'd do 10 benefits, he'd say "Yeah yeah, just call us, call us". And they finally got him to say "We can't do them all" so I think it was Sam or one of the guys told him "Somebody's gonna have to be manager, somebody's gonna have to be a bad guy". He said "We can't do it", and Scotty said "Well, I'll do it". So then I'd have to ask Scotty and we did a few things but you can't do them all. You know we tried to do the best we could but we just couldn't get around to doing all the free ones.

Q. Were you making money with Elvis back then?

No we never made any money, that wasn't the point. We were just trying to do something that we thought was gonna be a hit, cut good records – we didn't make a lot of money at all, it could have been a lot better but we had management problems and one thing and another so you can't argue with the

world so we'd just say "That's ok" and we were having a good time, we were young and doing pictures and TV shows, how many guys get the chance to do that.

Q. Shows, that's with Scotty, Bill and yourself?

Yeah, yeah

Q. There's loads of songs – do any of these songs stand out? Tell me about the studio recordings, did it take loads of times to do?

No not really once he got started sometimes they'd call a session here at the RCAB at 6 o'clock in the evening and he might not show up until 11 o'clock and then he'd sing, we'd all do round the piano, sing gospel for a couple more hours and all the higher ups were getting panicky spending a lot of money and that made them a little nervous. But once he got started he'd say "Ok guys time to go to work", and he was ready.

We'd listen to the acetate and everybody would take little notes of what you wanted to play in our own minds and he'd say "Well let's try it" and we'd kick it off and if he didn't like it he'd say "Well now let's do something else". It's a matter of hit and miss just whatever he thought what he wanted to hear that's what he got.

Q. Was there room for experimentation?

Yeah, nobody pushed us cos he wouldn't have allowed that in the first place. He'd say if everybody's uncomfortable and everybody's uptight we're not going to cut good records. If he felt the room was uptight "Knock it off guys – we'll get a bite to eat and take off for an hour or so then come back"

" I think I have something tonight that's not quite correct for evening wear. Blue suede shoes. "

Elvis Presley

Q. I read that you guys were being paid hourly so he'd make a joke with you just so you could make a few bucks?

Yeah well when we were doing the soundtracks for the pictures and he'd come around every now and again and say "Are you guys making any money yet" and we'd say "No Elvis cos it's going too fast".

You'd get paid by the hour in 3 hour segments and we'd say "No it's moving kinda fast" and he'd say "OK I'll take care of that" and he'd go to play the piano, go to sing gospel a couple of hours – they were still, the clock was still clicking you see and after a few hours I'd say "What do you think now?" and he'd say "OK we can get started again", you know.

And every so often he'd stop us "We'll take a break" but the clock was still ticking – he was good at that.

Q. Tell us about your roles in the movies and what you thought of his acting.

Well, our roles weren't much – none of us were actors. Bill wanted to be an actor, he really did. Bill could have been a good character actor he really could. None of us had any big lines or anything – Bill had a few, me and Scotty never did talk much on the scene itself, we just happened to be in a lot of scenes.

Bill had a couple of little acts that he did on Loving You. He did a good job, he could have been a good actor he sure could.

Q. How do you rate Scotty as a guitarist?

He was probably one of the finest guitar players you ever wanted to run into. The way he played was so unique from all the other guys, it was different. He played the thumb and the rhythm and just – if you could hear his records you could tell it's Scotty, there's no question about it. All the guitar players haven't figured out what he's doing yet.

Q. He's very modest when he comes to talking about himself?

Yeah, well he played some really good things on them records. And all the big guitar players, they talk about him all the time. How many good licks he played and his originality of what he was doing, they talk about him all the time.

Q. Do you think that Shake, Rattle and Roll was the world's first glimpse of Elvis on television?

Well, we had done a couple more songs before that I believe on one of those shows but I don't remember which one was which now.

Q. Why do you think his performances on television made such an impact?

Well he was different, absolutely different and his clothes were different. Like I said earlier, he was a good looking guy and that got all the ladies on his side of course and also he could sing and that was the main thing and the little band we had, the trio, was a good little trio. We played things that he needed so we stuck very close to his method of singing. He had a unique voice and all you had to do was just lay backand not do a lot and let him sing.

Q. Was his dancing and his lip snarl always there or did he have to develop that?

No, you know that dancing, when he first started he didn't dance around too much but a couple of times he was moving around a little bit and we got through and he said "Why are all those kids screaming and hollering" and we said "Well you're dancing, you're moving around" and he said "Oh am I?". I don't think he realised it. So after that he did more of it he could see the reaction in the kids by then and he said "Oh that's pretty good I'll just do some more".

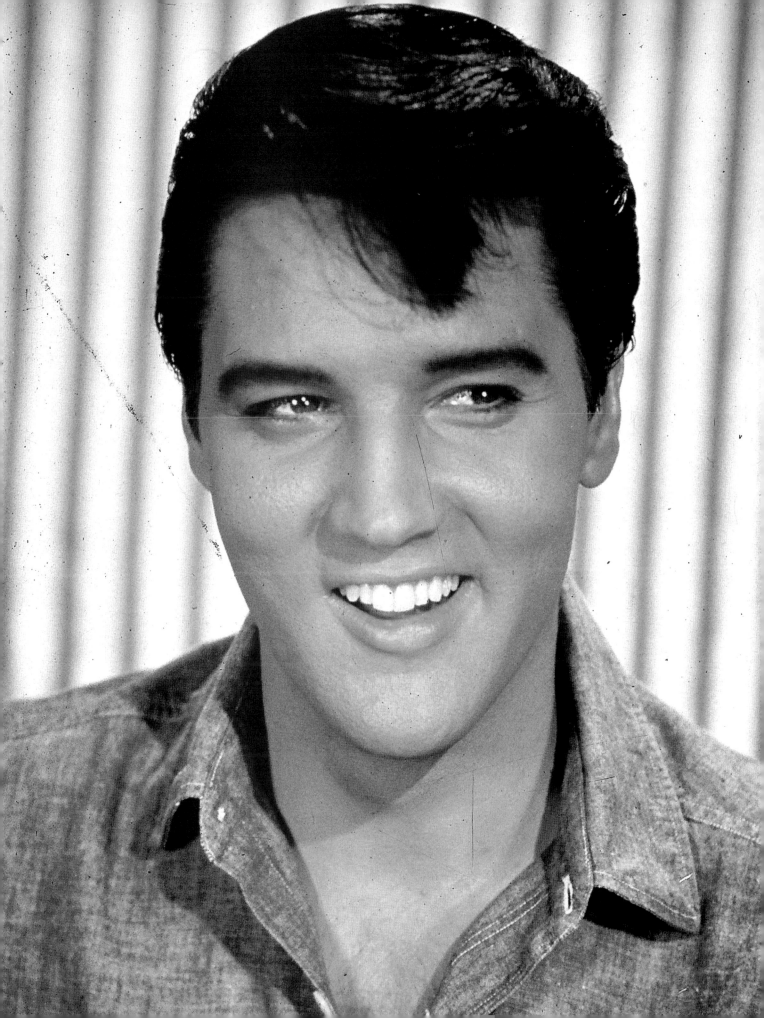

Q. Is it right that the song Hound Dog took 70 takes to complete?

No no no no, I don't know where they get that from but then they said 35, but actually what they were calling takes was a count of 1, 2, 3, 4 "No wrong tempo", or you play 2 or 3 bars then something would happen "No". They counted all those little stops and starts as a take. And I think he finally went back I'm not sure of the cut but it was way down on the 5th or 6th cut he took. But it wasn't nothing like 35 or 70 – I don't know where they got that from. They just counted all that stuff on tape.

Q. Can you or would you dispel any myths that are out there – is there any big myths that you can dispel, again like the one I've just said?

No not really – it's according to whose books you read of course. And I don't read them so I don't know who's writing what. I really don't pay that much attention to them. He treated me decent and he treated all of us decent so that's what we go by.

Q. How long did you play with Elvis and when did it end?

I was with him 14 years actually. Scotty and Bill they started it completely, those 3 guys were the band. I joined them a little bit later and a little bit later The Jordanaires joined us down in Atlanta, Georgia and they stayed with us a long time so it was just a matter of getting people that you could get along with actually.

Q. And tell us a bit about The Jordanaires – what did they bring to the music?

Well they helped us out a lot cos they were doing all the background parts, singing all the do-waps and to me it sounded like the horn section sometimes. They made it sound like we had a big band back there. Gordon played a little piano on some of the stage things and Hoyt Hawkins, he's passed away now, Hoyt played a little piano so it helped fill up the band.

Q. Do you think the early television performances were good in formal musical terms?

Yeah I think they were, I don't know how, what else we could have done. Course like I said they still had their big bands behind us and everything. But still we were doing like we were supposed to do and that's what they were buying.

Q. Do you think there was anything out of the ordinary in Elvis's version of Blue Suede Shoes and Tutti Frutti?

No. I listened to both Carl Perkins' and Elvis' and Carl had a superb version of it he really did, I think his was a little bit slower than ours but Elvis did a great job on it and Tutti Frutti he did a good job and I think he heard that from Little Richard – one of those guys had it out before we put it out. So, he was always listening to different artists and if he found a song he liked, he'd try it. And usually he was pretty good.

Q. Heartbreak Hotel, do you think that was the first real Elvis classic?

Yeah I think so – that was the record - that got him, that got him off of Sun actually. We were on Sun he wasn't and with the Heartbreak that was like, even before it was released I think it was like a million – that was the first million selling record for him which was pretty darn good. A new kid on the pike and there he is he's got a million seller.

Q. What did When the Blue Moon Turns to Gold tell us about Elvis' gospel influence?

He was great on the gospel song, I've always said that, and he loved gospel music. Every chance he got to hear a gospel group and he would go. Years they used to have several gospel troops come

through town all the time. And they played Memphis of course and he'd go back and see them, every one of them he knew all by heart, he knew them all by name and he just loved gospel music and that's where he got a lot of his feeling from.

Q. Did Love Me Tender provide the first real indicator of Elvis' talent as an interpreter of ballads?

Yeah, that was a good record, that Love Me Tender. For his first movie I thought it was pretty darn decent.

Q. Why do you think Elvis was such a phenomenon in the early days?

Well, he could sing, he was unusual – when he walked in a room you knew it was him. Like I said earlier he was a good looking guy so that might have been just a combination of all of it put together was probably what made it go so well.

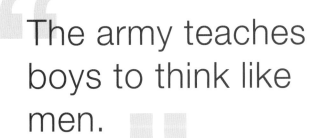

"The army teaches boys to think like men."

Elvis Presley

Q. Did Elvis' duet with Frank Sinatra demonstrate that the two were equals as performers?

I think they did a good job together. I think Sinatra kind of got on his side after a while, he wasn't sure about how they would like each other in other words. But they got on a show and they were laughing and grinning and having a good time in rehearsals and they all seemed like they really got along fine.

Q. Why was the '68 comeback special or was the comeback special Elvis at his very best do you think?

I think so – I think the whole show was good. The segment in the round was really good with the black little suit and all that stuff. No instruments, just Scotty's guitar and a couple of rhythm things. He looked good – that was the best I'd seen him look in a long time.

Q. With songs like My Way, was there a danger Elvis had become too showbiz? Was his version as good as Sinatra's?

I think it was. Sinatra had a great version and Elvis had a great version so I think it was a toss up between the two, it's according to who you liked the best. And some of the fans liked Sinatra and some liked Elvis. So it was a mixture of all of it and I thought that both cuts were good.

Q. What do you think were the musical highlights of Elvis' output in the 70's?

I wasn't around back then. You see I was gone in '68 so I can't answer those questions whatsoever. I thought that since he had to go to Vegas, he needed a show band, I mean he needed a production and that's what they were looking for and that's why he went over so well in Vegas.

Q. American Trilogy – the ultimate Elvis song do you think?

I think so, I like that song myself. Micky Newberry did a great job on it and Elvis sung the fire out of it. A lot of people out there in the audience, you'd see them on that split screen and you could see these people out there crying cos he was very sincere about it.

Q. Do the early 70s films of Elvis in concert do him justice as a performer?

Oh yeah, that's when he really got into the karate moves and the kicks and the big bands behind him and he really sounded good with that big band, he really did.

Q. Do you think Elvis was a perfectionist in terms of his performance?

Oh yeah, he wanted everything exactly right. Even on his records he wanted it right. He'd say "No we have to do it again". You gotta remember way back then we only had mono tracks so there weren't no fixing nothing, you'd go back in and do the whole song again so we just kept going.

Q. Aloha from Hawaii – the best example of a mature Elvis in concert?

That was another great concert but you know it's hard to say which one was the best cos there were all good. They made darn sure that he did a good job, course he made sure that he did a good job and the sound was good and the film was good and they all did great job – I can't say a darn thing bad about it.

Q. Do you think the 70s Vegas repertoire was sufficiently challenging?

No, no, he was doing basically his old songs except different tempos and I think he threw away a lot of the vocals on those up tempo when it got so fast that nobody could understand what he was talking about half of the time. I think he should have done them originally where they were and do more of them if he had to but don't just rush through them. No I don't think that's a good idea.

Q. Could the effect of Elvis' decline in health be seen in his later performances?

Well I didn't see him after a while anyhow. I knew that like everyone else you read the papers and you knew he was sick here and he was sick there. It seemed like every time he'd come to town he'd get sick and he ended up in the hospital and there was always something back and forth, it wasn't anything serious but it was just enough to figure he had been kind of not real well for the last few years.

Q. I mean, were drugs a problem when you worked with him?

No, never saw them. In fact he didn't drink. Me, Scotty and Bill, we'd have a beer or two you know and that was about it.

Q. Do you think Elvis was overrated or is he really the King in your opinion?

No he wasn't overrated by no means. He didn't like to be called the King but still he was the number 1 guy and he still is. I just got back from Denmark and Sweden and there's people over there that still love Elvis. Everywhere you go theylove Elvis, after all these years he's passed away.

Q. Do you remember where you were and how you felt when you heard he'd passed away?

I was at Sun Records actually, not Memphis but over at Belmont and Shelby Singleton had brought all this stuff out, all the Sun stuff and we were cutting somebody over there I don't remember who it was now and he came on the talkback about 4-4.30. He said "DJ" he said "We just heard Elvis had passed away" and he said "It's on the radio" he said "You want to call the session?"We were supposed to be through at 5 anyhow. I said "No, let's finish up". Costs a lot of money just to cancel a session you know, I said "No, no, we'll wait till 5 and then I'll run home". I didn't live too far from the studio at the time, maybe 10 minutes away. And I got on the phone and I tried to call everybody I knew, that was associated with

Elvis at that time. Couldn't get any, everybody was out of pocket. Everybody was either in the air coming or going. So finally I got hold of Joe Esposito at the house finally and he said it's true. So I caught the next plane out the next morning, me and my wife and the kids we went down and spent the whole day with them you know, at the home and the next morning I had to leave actually I had to go to Virginia – I had some more sessions up there so Billy Smith took me out the back gate, and back to the airport, me and the family and I got back home that night about 10 or 11 o'clock, so it was a sad, sad day for everybody.

Q. To sum up, is there anything you'd like to add about the whole time you were with Elvis and the whole time you were in the band?

Well the only thing is like I said, early on we all had a great time together. And I think the reason for that was we could all talk and sleep in the cars, stop and get a hamburger if you wanted to so that made it a little easier. As he got bigger and bigger and bigger, well we could feel that as we got bigger we couldn't get in the venues as easy.

We had to have certain passes, certain security and all that stuff. And it made it hard for everybody and we only saw him actually on stage and he's off stage. But early on it was all driving and stopping for food and one thing and another, we had a lot of time to talk.

Interview With Scotty Moore

Q. Tell me about when you first picked up the guitar, when you were in the Navy – tell me about your influences?

Well I guess I started trying to play a little bit when I was around 9 or 10 years old, I got interested in it. I had three brothers, my three brothers and my dad all played string instruments and there was 14 years difference between me and the next one up the ladder. And so by the time I got to that age, everybody was gone, married or in the navy or whatever and I think one thing drove me was just being hard headed more than anything else

Q. And what kind of music were you interested in?

Any kind, it didn't matter. Course I heard a lot of country music back, coming off the farm and a lot of black music and I heard some popular music of course on the radio and stuff like that.

Q. You have quite a unique style. How did you develop that unique style?

Just stealing from everybody I guess and putting it all together. If I've got a style - I never considered that I did. I tried to play the song, I tried to listen to the song cos I don't read music or at least as Chet Atkins used to say "You didn't read enough to hurt your playing." I tried to listen to a song and play something I'd think would fit the music or the way the guy was singing, you know, that way.

Q. When did you first get involved with working with Elvis? When did you first meet him and what were your first impressions of him?

Well I had a group of my own in Memphis called The Starlite Wranglers, which I had formed right after I had got out of the navy and we did one record at Sun and, when I found out there was a place there where you could make records, I went in and talked to Sam Phillips. He agreed to listen to the group and

we went in and auditioned for him and at first, I always remember, the first thing he said was "Have you got any original material?" and we said "No." And he said "Well you got a good group, I like the group.

If you get some original material, come back, I'd like to see what you got."And so me and my oldest brother and Doug Poindexter, we wrote 2 songs just over a few days and we went back and we did the record with Sam which he put out and we sold maybe 10 or 12, one of those kind of deals, but from all that Sam and I became good friends.

The job I had I was through work probably 2 or 3 o'clock in the afternoon and I'd drive by the studio and if he wasn't tied up working well we'd go next door to Miss Taylor's restaurant and drink coffee and just chit chat about the business and "What do you think?" and "What do you think we need to do?" just in general and one day we were having coffee and his secretary was there, Miss Marion Keisker was with us and she asked Sam "Did you ever talk to that boy that was in here about a year ago that cut that demo for his mother's .." she gave the details and he said "No."

So I'd say about probably a week or two went by and every day that went by and I saw him and be there having coffee together I'd always ask him "Oh by the way did you ever contact that boy?" cos I kept that in my mind.

So finally one day Marion again was having coffee with us and he turned to her and asked her and… I said "I haven't even heard this guy's name yet, even", and he turned to Marion and says "Get that guy, have you still got his telephone number?" She says "Yeah" and he said "Give it to Scotty" and he turned to me and said "You call him and ask him to come over to your house and see what you think." And that was fine. So in a little bit Marion goes and comes back and gives me the piece of paper with his number on it and I looked at it and I say "His

name – Elvis Presley – what kind of a name is that?" And that was really all that was said and goodbye.

When I got home that afternoon I called and his mother answered and she said that he was at the theatre I believe and that she'd have him call when he got back. So a couple of hours later he called and I told him that I was working with Sam Phillips and he was looking for material, looking for artists blah, blah and would he be interested in doing an audition and he said "Well sure."

And I asked him to come over to my house, which was on Bill's Avenue, the next day which was July the, Sunday would have been the 4th, no 3rd, no 4th cos Memphis didn't shoot fireworks on Sunday but Sunday they did actually celebrate it on next day on Monday, that's the way it went.

He came over that Sunday and he sat around and he played and sang everything, it seemed like he knew every song in the world and, but he didn't know how to play half of them. But he'd play along and when he didn't know the chords he'd just keep playing, keep singing. And this went on for a couple of hours. Bill Black at that time, he lived just a few doors down the street from me and he came down to sit in, just listening with us for a little while and left. Then when Elvis left I told Elvis I said "Either I or Sam will probably be calling you about coming into the studio".

I called Sam and I told him I said "Well it seems like the boy knows all the songs. Being as young as he is he's got a good voice", and Sam said "Well I'll call him and ask him to come in tomorrow night", which would have been Monday night and said "Can you and Bill come in and do a little background? I don't want the whole band, I just need a little noise behind him to see what he sounds like".

And we said "Sure." Bill came back down and I asked Bill, I said "Bill what did you think of him?"

And he said "Alright - seems like a new bunch of songs, he sounds pretty good you know? Had good timing", and so forth, that kind of thing. And so we went down to the studio the next night, Monday night and there again, he went through all these different songs, just whatever came to mind, Sam didn't request anything or anything. It was at least 10 o'clock, it was getting late, we were about ready to go to the house cos it was still just an audition.

And Elvis stood up and started playing his guitar and singing That's Alright and Bill started slapping his bass and playing along with him. I had never heard the song, Bill had never heard it and I took the guitar and started playing, looking for something, we were just jamming.

The door to the control room was open and Sam stuck his head out and said "What are you guys doing?" We said "we're just goofing around" and he said "Well just do it a little more". Cos the mikes weren't on or anything and he said "Let me go and turn the mikes on" or whatever and we got on the mike, went through it 2 or 3 times and that was it. Lord am I glad or am I sorry, I don't know!

Q. So tell me a bit about The Blue Moon Boys and your fellow musicians Bill and DJ?

Well Blue Moon Boys was just Bill and myself. They dropped that name when we left Sun. DJ never recorded with us. We started using DJ when we went to the Louisiana Hayride and he did a lot of shows with us during the period we were on Sun.

Heartbreak Hotel was the first thing he played on when we came to Nashville to RCA.

Q. Did the phenomenon with rock and roll happen overnight or did it slowly happen?

Well, actually the first thing is – what is rock and roll? Alan Freed had a disc jockey show up in, where was he? He was the one that coined that phrase. I suppose everybody knows really what the term really means – it came from black music and they would use that term to get across their message. I don't know, that name did stick when he started calling it rock and roll. Before that Elvis was being called the Hillbilly Cat, Rockabilly – gosh I don't know what else they called him.

I'm sure he had some good names. But for us, as far as the band, we just enjoyed playing – there wasn't a producer, there wasn't somebody who said you gotta play something this way or that way – they let us do what we wanted to do.
Q. What happened after that? Did you start working with Elvis full time? When did you also become his manager?

Well the first thing, the group I was telling you about that I had, The Starlite Wranglers, we were doing a Friday and Saturday gig at a small club here in town, Bel Air Club, and that was the first thing after we cut That's Alright – then a few days went by and we finally came up with the B-side and that came up in really the same way, cos we went back in a couple of days later and Elvis started going through all different songs.

Sam would think of something or I would think of something and he'd try it "Do you know so and so?" "Yeah I know it" – and he'd try something else just to.

Bill was sitting on his bass fiddle, I don't know, if you have a bass just laying on the floor and he was sitting, just sitting on it and he started beating on it and singing Blue Moon of Kentucky which was a waltz country song by Bill Monroe and he was singing it in falsetto, high tenor you know, up tempo and Elvis knew the song and he started singing along with him. That was the B side, it was that simple.

Q. When you were in the studio, how many takes would it take to do songs?

Well, once we landed on something that he knew and liked, it might have been something that Sam had put out before or whatever – but when he liked the song and everything, well it didn't take us too long. He might miss a word, I might miss a chord, Sam would goof sometimes when we were recording, but we're talking about skin of your teeth back in those days, but once we'd got everything in order, it didn't take too many takes. It was just mainly – when he was satisfied that he'd done his best singing, it was the main thing.

Q. Was he a perfectionist?

It was the feel, he wanted to feel, we all felt the same way, if I might have missed a note or not hit a note perfect, if the total thing felt good, that's what counted. I mean I might have played something fantastic and I would never have played the same thing twice anyway but when I played if it felt good, it was the same thing. Elvis was the same way.

Q. Can you tell us a bit about where we are now?

Well, we're in RCAB in Nashville. We cut a few things here. Course I guess most of our recording was done in California and some of the hits were done, a few were done in New York too. But all the time I was with him, we did several of them here.

Q. Tell us about how you became his manager and what that relationship was like?

Well after we put out that first record, of course the local DJs around Memphis started getting calls and everything. A couple of other people that were "music managers" and what have you and everybody was calling him. The three of us – Bill, Sam, myself and Elvis - were all just sitting chatting one day and he was talking about the people calling him and he said "Well I don't know what to tell them". And it was actuallySam's idea he said "Well I'll tell you what.

Scotty, why don't you sign up as manager for a year and it'll give us time to look for somebody that we all trust and want to work with."And that's the way it happened and of course, we had Bob Neil came in, who was a local disc jockey and he started booking

us in and around Memphis, Arkansas, Mississippi, locally – cos he was on a radio station, I think he was on about 6 o'clock in the morning and at that time in the morning the station really went out.

Q. What was life on the road like?

Starting off like that, none of us had ever been on the road so number one you'd have an experience and then pretty soon you'd start to get tired and say will this never end. And yet tomorrow the next show will be better, there'll be a better show, there'll be more money, it'll be, you know, everything is supposed to go up. But we were just typical, like, I won't say like any other band that's out there but – we'd have our fusses and everything. Bill and I did most of the driving in the early days then when DJ joined us, he did some of the driving too.

We had a problem with Elvis when he was driving – he was a good driver, a very good driver – but for some reason he just could not read road signs. If

you came to a fork in the road, well, he'd take the wrong one every time. But he was a good driver. DJ was a good driver. We were on the road when they were just starting to build interstates and we left Memphis going – I don't know where we were going – but, we got to St Louis where they had just built the brand new ring road around, and it was around 11 o'clock at night or something like that.

I had been driving and I turned it over to DJ and got over in the other seat and went to sleep. Bill and Elvis were in the back seat. I woke up in daylight, sitting on the side of the road, still asleep and I said "Where are we at?" and he says "Still in St Louis." He said "I can't get off this damn road."We never let him forget it either. He'll probably bring it up.

Q. What was the music scene like when you went to the live events?

In the very, very, very early days when Bob Naylor was booking us, we were doing a lot of little country schoolhouses, I say country schoolhouses cos they were little towns and the schoolhouses would be outside of the city limits maybe. And say the show was starting at 7 o'clock we would get there at 7.30 and there wouldn't be a soul anywhere. And you had to take your own PAs – I mean they had PAs in those little places like that, it was just had a microphone that sometimes just plugged into my little amplifier. There wasn't even any equipment there – you'd take all of that.

We were the whole show and we started getting some other people to go with us. Arnie Wheeler was a country artist back then – he went with us on a lot. But anyway, we would get there about 7.30, and get set up, 8 o'clock doors open and just whoof! every body was there.

Well, they'd heard the record on the radio but they hadn't seen him. And they were just sitting.Well Bill started cutting up cos the bass player back in those days, especially on country acts, the bass player

always had to dress up in, be a clown but he started whooping and hollering, sitting on the bass, riding the bass and just cutting up you know.

And the people would start coming alive by watching him and then they would get into the music and that's what really got him started. I mean he, and everything he'd do, they'd clap and carry on and he'd embellish on it.

Q. And had he always had those dance moves and the lip snarl or did that come later?

The only thing that he had natural that I know of was the first thing we did at the Overton Park Shell that was the first actual stage performance in front of an audience and Bob Naylor got us on that as a closing, actually as an extra act – Slim Whitman was the featured singer on that.

And for me the guitar player, if he's standing up, usually will either pat his foot, keep in time or sit down and if he doesn't do it he doesn't do anything. But Elvis, when he was singing and playing he'd always raise up on the balls of his feet, both feet. And with the big breeches legs back then, they started flapping and he looked like he was really getting going with it. And that was what they were really laughing about, going on about.

Q. Is there any myths you want to dispel about anything that's out there in the media?

If you could name them, I could tell you a whole bunch of them but they just don't come right to mind.

Q. I had June 27th – was that another meeting?

July 4th was the first day I met him – I talked to him on the phone the day before. Of course I found out much later that he had been in Sun before and had done some of those little demos supposedly for his mother. But he had never mentioned that.

Q. So when was the turning point where Sun and RCA came in there? When did that change?

There was '54/'55 were the Sun sessions, we discussed those.

Q. When did you guys go from Sun to RCA?

Well, there had been several people trying to buy us contracts and Parker came into the deal and set the whole thing up with RCA and they paid Sam the money. And this was when we went to RCA and cut the first record.

Q. And can you tell us a bit about that?

Well, it was just another studio date we did it at Trafco. Their building was down on McGavock Street and in the lower floor RCA had rented the studio and that's where we cut Heartbreak Hotel.

Q. Tell me, what were your feelings about Colonel Parker and that change in management? What did you make of that?

Well, I probably don't want to get into that.

Q. OK, tell me about the movies. I heard you were in a couple of the movies. What did you make of the soundtracks?

We did a couple of the early ones with him as extras. Well it was actually the band in one, the first one – I always say the first one, we weren't in – that was interesting.We went out to – when he did Love Me Tender – they took The Jordanaires, Bill, DJ, myself and Elvis they had us all come out to a bungalow on the lot at MGM and it was all pre set-up, we knew that later, cos Elvis didn't know anything either about it.

You've seen the movie, you know what it was about. So we go into our regular show we're doing on the tour. And they said "No that's not the kind of music we want, sorry." "That was ok thank you very much". Then we see the movie and we've been playing hillbilly music all our lives. But it was set up – Ken Derby, who was the musical director, he had his own guys he wanted to use. I understand those kind of things. It wasn't bad, you just knew it was pre-done.

Q. What did you make of Elvis as an actor?

I just wish he could have got some real scripts later on. When they found out they could make some money off of him, I guess, well, he went ahead and did it – I never will understand why. He just wouldn't put his foot down on management and say "I will not do this. Give me something." He did have a chance at A Star is Born – they had that in mind for him, and then Parker wouldn't let him do it.

Q. What did you think of Elvis as a person?

Well, he was just a regular guy. With all the stuff that hit him at such an early age and so fast - he never really had a chance to grow up. He always had his so-called friends around him and he just never grew up.

> Since the beginning, it was just the same. The only difference, the crowds are bigger now.

Elvis Presley

81

Q. Cos I was going to ask you about the money, it's fascinating, but if you don't want to talk about it?

That happened here by the way. Yes, he cut that song here in…… yeah, I think Jerry Reed wrote and played on.

Q. Do you think that early on drugs were affecting Elvis in the early years?

It didn't affect his music really at the time that I was with him. He didn't really get into that, that started when he was in the army, he started taking binnies. I think they used to give them when they were going out on manoeuvres because he was driving a tank. It used to keep you awake and that was the normal thing. But I guess he got to liking them pretty good and then went onto different stuff. I don't know really all the background on that just what I read.

Q. What did you think of The Jordanaires and what did they bring to the Elvis sound?

What can you say, when he found a group he liked and he liked The Jordanaires from even before he'd ever recorded with them so it was just natural that they would work with him. They still sound good, you know.

Q. Where do you think Elvis got a lot of his influence?

Mostly from religion music. He loved quartets, he loved The Jordanaires, The Blackwood Brothers, just the way he was raised, he used to go to all night singings and such. I guess that's where he first met The Jordanaires maybe – he met them in Memphis - they were there on a show I think.

Q. What about your guitars, what did you use back then?

On the first record I had an ES-295, Gibson ES-295. And when I first came out of the navy I bought a

Fender and, mainly because in the navy there were a couple of other guys on there who played a little bit, and we'd bought Japanese guitars when going to port and the frets were made out of beer cans cos you'd wear the frets out in 30 days. But we were always sitting down so they were thin guitars, like Fenders, call them copies of Fenders.

And when I came out I bought a Fender but then standing up I couldn't keep it still, it kept getting away from me. And I was walking down town one day by the music store and they had just put one of the ES-295s in there which was gold coloured and all the hardware was gold-plated and everything and I said "I gotta have it."

And I went in and made a trade and got that, and that's what I had when we first got started. I kept it through the first 4 records.

On the 5th record I got an EchoSonic amplifier which had an echo in it that, I'd heard this on one record by Chet Atkins and my thought was that if I had that – cos I was always worried we'd do something and when Sam was using the slapback echo on the whole song, that when we went out to do the show it would sound lah, you know, it didn't have the pep then.

And I knew that if I could get that amplifier then at least one instrument would have the right sound. And I called Nashville and I don't remember who I talked to now but I found out somehow or another from chat that Ray Butts was in Cairo, Illinois, a music store that had designed this amp and I drove up there to see him and he said "Yeah, be glad to build you one." Now this is 1954 and it only cost $500 for that amplifier. I still have it.

Q. Shake, Rattle and Roll – was this the world's first glimpse of Elvis?

Yeah, probably so. They might have heard the name. Yeah.

Q. Hound Dog – can you describe what made the early Elvis sound unique in musical terms?

There again, we just did what we felt. We only had 3 Jordanaires on that. Gordon Stoker was playing piano cos Shorty Long had another gig he had to go to he was working on a stage show and so he had to leave. And Gordon took over piano and so we just had the 3 Jordanaires singing on that. And you can tell it if you listen to it real close with a musical ear. I'm trying to be real nice about Tez. But let me interject this, when everything got that it felt good for everybody, that was the cut.

Q. Do you think the early television performances were good in musical terms?

No, because they could have been so much better, you weren't allowed to, you couldn't set a mike in front, you couldn't dare see a microphone then or anything, the mike was probably way up in the air. You know how television used to be. Now they finally got away from that – ok, you're playing the guitar or what, let me see it.

Q. They used to put the drummer behind the curtain?

Yeah, oh yeah. DJ used to play at the Hayride, that's when we first met him – he was playing behind a screen. There was a shadow, you could see the shadow but you didn't see him. Now you don't wanna see him!

Q. Do you think the guitar breaks were important in the early arrangements?

Well, I don't know if they would have been important or not. They were just of the style of the day, as it has always been. A singer will sing a verse or two, then whether it's the guitar or a piano or whatever it is then the instrumental pad goes in there too. Better leave that up to the beholding of the people listening I guess.

Q. Was there anything out of the ordinary in Elvis' version of Blue Suede Shoes and Tutti Frutti that was better than the original renditions?

Just that we did them probably faster maybe.Again we just did it the way we felt it. RCA, Steve Scholes whatever had been trying to get, when Carl's record was doing real good, they'd been trying to get Elvis to cover it and Elvis wouldn't do it.
He said "No, I'm not going to cover it, cos Carl's a friend of mine, we work the shows together", and so forth.We were going to New York, I can't remember which show we were going to be on. But Carl had one also up there and they'd had, that's when Carl had the wreck and Bill, DJ and myself were on our way up to there and we were.

We went by to see Carl in the hospital and they all said send him a telegram or call in with something also. But he was already in New York. And when we got to New York he said he wanted to do Blue Suede Shoes on the show. He was doing it for Carl, you know, he wasn't trying to take away anything. Cos they had been pushing him trying to get him to do it before Carl had the wreck.

Q. Do you think Heartbreak Hotel was the first real Elvis classic?

Well, yeah cos it was the first record on RCA and of course it had been the first one that was played all over the whole country. Before that it was strictly a southern regional hit kind of thing.

Q. And Suspicious Minds – was this the perfect repertoire for Elvis? Did it sum up what was happening in his life at the time?

No, I never thought of it that way. I don't know. Could be.

Q. American Trilogy – the ultimate Elvis song?

See that was done originally by Micky Newberry.

Elvis had heard it. I think he believed it was just a good show tune to do on stage and maybe make some people stand up straighter and salute or so – political type thing you know.

Q. Do you think he was a perfectionist in terms of his performances, Elvis?

Well a perfectionist you never knew what he was going to do. I mean when he went on stage you didn't know what he was going to do. There was perfection maybe in his own way and how he was going to do something but we didn't know what he was going to do.

Q. Could the effect of Elvis' decline in health be seen in his later performances do you think?

Well, the only time I saw him was when he was on video or something. The last time I saw him, I can't remember what the show was, where he had gained so much weight and I could tell there was something wrong but I didn't know what.

Q. Can you remember where you were when he passed away and what your feelings were?

Yeah, I was in the control room at Monument Studios doing some editing as such.

Q. And how did you feel?

I don't know, well I guess just saddened of course.

Q. Do you think Elvis is overrated or do you think he's the king?

He wouldn't have liked the title king, I know that for sure. If we could break everything down, he would be underrated in some things and he'd be overrated in other things. So I'd just leave that to the individual.

Q. What about the book? Can you mention anything about the book and how that came about?

Jim Dickerson was the one that did the book on me. He'd just been pestering me to do it and I finally gave in – that's all I know.

Q. Did your daughter have something to do with that?

Yeah, our daughter was friends of his and that came about in a roundabout way, Vicky.

Q. Is there anything you might like to add?

No I'm fine if you've got enough. The book had been out of print for some time but they've done another printing and brought it up to date, added another chapter about all my illnesses and hospital stays and such mostly.

Q. Are you ok now?

Yeah, I got a couple of nice holes in my head. I guess so.

Q. Do you pick up the guitar now?

Yeah, I still try to play a little bit. I'm still having trouble with my right arm and hand but part of that's just pure age, arthritis.

Q. And if I were to say that your guitar playing was a major role in the history of American popular music, what would you say?

Thank you!

Elvis Presley Did you Know?

Elvis had a twin. On January 8, 1935, Elvis Aron (later spelled Aaron) Presley was born at his parents' two-room house in East Tupelo, Mississippi, about 35 minutes after his identical twin brother, Jesse Garon, who was stillborn. The next day, Jesse was buried in an unmarked grave in nearby Priceville Cemetery. The Young Elvis. Until his teens, Elvis was blonde, before his hair turned brown. Elvis died his hair black Elvis First Show.

On 30 July 1954, Elvis played one of his first shows, at the Overton Park Shell in Memphis. He was, apparently, so nervous, that his legs started to shake. The outlandish flares the singer had chosen to wear that evening only exacerbated the shaky movement. The girls in the audience went wild, and Elvis decided to incorporate his shaky-legs routine into future shows.

Elvis On The Radio.

Elvis's first radio play was on Memphis station WHBQ, on the Red, Hot and Blue Right", Show, in 1954. DJ Dewey Phillips played "That's All and, a week later Sun Records had received 6,000 advance orders for the single "That's All Right"/ "Blue Moon of Kentucky".

Ambition is a dream with a V8 engine

Elvis Presley

Elvis Breakthrough.

Elvis's national breakthrough was the 1956 release of Heartbreak Hotel, inspired by a newspaper report of a suicide.

Elvis bought Graceland when he was 22. In 1957, Elvis shelled out $102,500 for Graceland, the Memphis mansion that served as his home base for two decades. Situated on nearly 14 acres, it was built in 1939 by Dr. Thomas Moore and his wife Ruth on land that once was part of a 500-acre farm dubbed Graceland in honor of the original owner's daughter, Grace, who was Ruth Moore's great-aunt.

The Moores' white-columned home also came to be known as Graceland, and when Elvis purchased the place he kept the name. Elvis' controversial manager, Colonel Tom Parker, was a former carnival barker.

Born Andreas Cornelis van Kuijk in the Netherlands in 1909, Elvis's future manager immigrated illegally to America as a young man, where he reinvented himself as Tom Parker and claimed to be from West Virginia (his true origins weren't known publicly until the 1980s). He worked as a pitchman for traveling carnivals, followed by stints as dog catcher and pet cemetery founder, among other occupations, then managed the careers of several country music singers. In 1948, Parker finagled the honorary title of colonel from the governor of Louisiana and henceforth insisted on being referred to as the Colonel.

Elvis bought Franklin Roosevelt's presidential yacht. In 1964, Elvis paid $55,000 for the Potomac, the 165-foot-long vessel that served as FDR's "floating White House" from 1936 to 1945. Constructed in 1934, the Potomac originally was a U.S. Coast Guard cutter.

After the president's death in 1945, the ship was decommissioned and had a series of owners before Elvis bought it. However, he soon donated it to St. Jude's Children's Hospital, which in turn sold the vessel to raise money. (In 1980, the Potomac, then being used by drug smugglers, was seized in San Francisco by U.S. Customs. It later was restored and opened to the public.)

The Karate King

Elvis was a black belt in karate. He took up martial arts under the shotokan sensei Jürgen Seydal, while fulfilling his military duties in Germany in 1958. He was awarded his black belt before he returned to the United States, in 1960, by the chito-ryu instructor Hank Slemansky.

Elvis meets The President.

On 21 December 1970, Presley met President Nixon at the White House. Presley had initiated the meeting with a six-page letter to the President, in which he had spelt out his desire to be made a "Federal Agent-at-Large" in the Bureau of Narcotics and Dangerous Drugs. During his meeting with Nixon, Presley denounced The Beatles as being 'un-American' for their open drug-taking and anti-Vietnam politics. For his part, Nixon reminded Presley of his need to "retain credibility". Nevertheless, he is said to have given Presley a 'Special Agent' badge.

Elvis in Concert.

He only performed five concerts outside the United States - all in Canada in 1957. At the time of his death, he was planning a European tour. He only set foot on British soil once, when the plane taking him back to the United States from Germany stopped to refuel at Glasgow Prestwick airport. The singer enjoyed a two-hour stopover before re-boarding the military plane. Almost 6ft Tall! Elvis was 5ft 11.75in (182 cm); however, he routinely wore shoes that had "lifts" inserted into his size 11 shoes making him over 6 feet tall.

Off The Stage.

Elvis's favourite hobbies were go-carting, karate, touch football, gospel singing, numerology.

Grammy Awards.

Elvis won three Grammy Awards - his three Grammy wins, incidentally, were all for gospel recordings: the 1967 album, "How Great Thou Art;" the 1974 live recording of the song, "How Great Thou Art;" and a Grammy for his 1972 album, "He Touched Me."

Elvis In The Army

While in the Army Elvis bought his fellow soldiers clothes and TVs and gave his army pay to charity. Elvis The Last Concert
* His last concert was at the Market Square Arena in Indianapolis, Indiana, on June 26th 1977. His last song at the concert was Can't Help Falling In Love With You. "Way Down" recorded in October 1976, it was Elvis's last single released before his death on August 16th 1977..

Elvis Presley Albums 1956 - 1977

ELVIS PRESLEY - 1956

Blue Suede Shoes
I'm Countin' on You
I Got a Woman
One-sided Love Affair
I Love You Because
Just Because
Tutti Frutti
Tryin' to Get to You
I'm Gonna Sit Right down and Cry
I'll Never Let You Go
Blue Moon
Money Honey

"Rock and roll music, if you like it, if you feel it, you can't help but move to it. That's what happens to me. I can't help it.

Elvis Presley

ELVIS

Rip It Up
Love Me
When My Blue Moon Turns to Gold Again
Long Tall Sally
First in Line
Paralyzed
So Glad You're Mine
Old Shep
Ready Teddy
Anyplace Is Paradise
How's the World Treating You
How Do You Think I Feel

LOVING YOU - 1957

Mean Woman Blues
Teddy Bear
Loving You
Got a Lot o' Livin' to Do
Lonesome Cowboy
Hot Dog
Party
Blueberry Hill
True Love
Don't Leave Me Now
Have I Told You Lately that I Love You
I Need You So

ELVIS' CHRISTMAS ALBUM

Santa Claus Is Back in Town
White Christmas
Here Comes Santa Claus
I'll Be Home for Christmas
Blue Christmas
Santa Bring My Baby Back to Me
O Little Town of Bethlehem
Silent Night
Peace in the Valley
I Believe
Take My Hand, Precious Lord
It Is No Secret

ELVIS' GOLDEN RECORDS, VOL. 1 - 1958

Hound Dog
Loving You
All Shook Up
Heartbreak Hotel
Jailhouse Rock
Love Me
Too Much
Don't Be Cruel
That's When Your Heartaches Begin
Teddy Bear
Love Me Tender
Treat Me Nice
Anyway You Want Me
I Want You, I Need You, I Love You

KING CREOLE

As long as I have you
Hard headed woman
Trouble
Steadfast, loyal and true
Dixieland rock
Don't ask me why
Lover doll
Crawfish
Young dreams
New Orleans

FOR LP FANS ONLY

That's All Right, Mama
Lawdy Miss Clawdy
Mystery Train
Playing for Keeps
Poor Boy
My Baby Left Me
I Was the One
Shake, Rattle and Roll
I'm Left, You're Right, She's Gone
You're a Heartbreaker
Blue Suede Shoes

A DATE WITH ELVIS - 1959

Blue Moon of Kentucky
Young and Beautiful
Baby I Don't Care
Milkcow Blues Boogie
Baby, Let's Play House
Good Rockin' Tonight
Is It So Strange
We're Gonna Move
I Want to Be Free
I Forgot to Remember to Forget

ELVIS' GOLD RECORDS, VOL. 2
(50,000,000 Elvis Fans Can't Be Wrong)(LPM 2075)

I Need Your Love Tonight
Don't
Wear My Ring Around Your Neck
My Wish Came True
I Got Stung
One Night
A Big Hunk o' Love
I Beg of You
A Fool Such as I
Doncha' Think It's Time

ELVIS IS BACK - 1960

Make Me Know It
Fever
The Girl of My Best Friend
I Will Be Home Again
Dirty, Dirty Feeling
Thrill of Your Love
Soldier Boy
Such a Night
It Feels So Right
Girl Next Door Went A'walking
Like a Baby
Reconsider Baby

G.I. BLUES

Tonight Is So Right For Love
What's She Really Like
Frankfort Special
Wooden Heart
G.I. Blues
Pocketful of Rainbows
Shoppin' Around
Big Boots
Didja' Ever
Blue Suede Shoes
Doin' the Best I Can

HIS HAND IN MINE

His Hand in Mine
I'm Gonna Walk Dem Golden Stairs
In My Father's House
Milky White Way
Known Only to Him
I Believe in the Man in the Sky
Joshua Fit the Battle
He Knows Just What I Need
Swing Down Sweet Chariot
Mansion over the Hilltop
If We Never Meet Again
Working on the Building

SOMETHING FOR EVERYBODY - 1961

There's Always Me
Give Me the Right
It's a Sin
Sentimental Me
Starting Today
Gently
I'm Coming Home
In Your Arms
Put the Blame on Me
Judy
I Want You with Me
I Slipped, I Stumbled, I Fell

BLUE HAWAII

Blue Hawaii
Almost Always True
Aloha Oe
No More
Can't Help Falling in Love
Rock-a-hula Baby
Moonlight Swim
Ku-u-i-po
Ito Eats
Slicin' Sand
Hawaiian Sunset
Beach Boy Blues
Island of Love
Hawaiian Wedding Song

POT LUCK - 1962

Kiss Me Quick
Just for Old Time Sake
Gonna Get Back Home Somehow
Easy Question
Steppin' out of Line
I'm Yours
Something Blue
Suspicion
I Feel that I've Known You Forever
Night Rider
Fountain of Love
That's Someone You Never Forget

> "I'm trying to keep a level head. You have to be careful out in the world. It's so easy to get turned."
>
> Elvis Presley

GIRLS! GIRLS! GIRLS!

Girls! Girls! Girls!
I Don't Wanna Be Tied
Where Do You Come From?
I Don't Want To
We'll Be Together
A Boy Like Me, a Girl Like You
Earth Boy
Return to Sender
Because of Love
Thanks to the Rolling Sea
Song of the Shrimp
The Walls Have Ears
We're Coming in Loaded

IT HAPPENED AT THE WORLDS FAIR - 1963

Beyond the Bend
Relax
Take Me to the Fair
They Remind Me Too Much of You
One Broken Heart for Sale
I'm Falling in Love Tonight
Cotton Candy Land
A World of Our Own
How Would You Like to Be?
Happy Ending

ELVIS' GOLDEN RECORDS, VOL. 3

It's Now or Never
Stuck on You
Fame and Fortune
I Gotta Know
Surrender
I Feel So Bad
Are You Lonesome Tonight
His Latest Flame
Little Sister
Good Luck Charm
Anything that's Part of You
She's Not You

FUN IN ACAPULCO

Fun in Acapulco
Vino, Dinero y Amor
Mexico
El Toro
Marguerita
The Bullfighter Was a Lady
No Room to Rhumba in a Sports Car
I Think I'm Gonna Like It Here
Bossa Nova, Baby
You Can't Say No in Acapulco
Guadalajara
Love Me Tonight
Slowly but Surely

KISSIN' COUSINS - 1964

Kissin' Cousins
Smokey Mountain Boy
There's Gold in the Mountains
One Boy Two Little Girls
Catchin' on Fast
Tender Feeling
Anyone
Barefoot Ballad
Once Is Enough
Kissin' Cousins
Echoes of Love
Long Lonely Highway

ROUSTABOUT

Roustabout
Little Egypt
Poison Ivy League
Hard Knocks
It's a Wonderful World
Big Love Big Heartache
One Track Heart
It's Carnival Time
Carny Town
There's a Brand New Day on the Horizon
Wheels on My Heels

GIRL HAPPY - 1965

Girl Happy
Spring Fever
Fort Lauderdale Chamber of Commerce
Startin' Tonight
Wolf Call
Do Not Disturb
Cross My Heart and Hope to Die
The Meanest Girl in Town
Do the Clam
Puppet on a String
I've Got to Find My Baby
You'll Be Gone

ELVIS FOR EVERYONE

Your Cheatin' Heart
Summer Kisses, Winter Tears
Finders Keepers, Losers Weepers
In My Way
Tomorrow Night
Memphis Tennessee
For the Millionth and the Last Time
Forget Me Never
Sound Advice
Santa Lucia
I Met Her Today
When It Rains, It Really Pours

HARUM SCARUM

Harem Holiday
My Desert Serenade
Go East, Young Man
Mirage
Kismet
Shake that Tambourine
Hey Little Girl
Golden Coins
So Close, Yet So Far
Animal Instinct
Wisdom of the Ages

FRANKIE AND JOHNNY - 1966

Frankie and Johnny
Come Along
Petunia the Gardener's Daughter
Chesay
What Every Woman Lives For
Look out Broadway
Beginner's Luck
Down by the Riverside and When the Saints Come
Marchin' In
Shout It Out
Hard Luck
Please Don't Stop Loving Me
Everybody Come Aboard

PARADISE HAWAIIAN STYLE

Paradise, Hawaiian Style
Queenie Wahine's Papaya
Scratch My Back
Drums of the Islands
Datin'
A Dog's Life
House of Sand
Stop Where You Are
This Is My Heaven
Sand Castles

SPINOUT

Stop Look and Listen
Adam and Evil
All that I Am
Never Say Yes
Am I Ready
Beach Shack
Spinout
Smorgasbord
I'll Be Back
Tomorrow Is a Long Time
Down in the Alley
I'll Remember You

HOW GREAT THOU ART - 1967

How Great Thou Art
In the Garden
Somebody Bigger Than You and I
Farther Along
Stand by Me
Without Him
So High
Where Could I Go but to the Lord
By and By
If the Lord Wasn't Walking by my Side
Run On
Where No One Stands Alone
Crying in the Chapel

DOUBLE TROUBLE

Double Trouble
Baby, if You'll Give Me All of Your Love
Could I Fall in Love
Long Legged Girl
City by Night
Old MacDonald
I Love Only One Girl
There is So Much World to See
It Won't Be Long
Never Ending
Blue River
What Now, What Next, Where To

CLAMBAKE

Clambake
Who Needs Money
A House that Has Everything
Confidence
Hey, Hey, Hey
You Don't Know Me
The Girl I Never Loved
How Can You Lose What You Never Had
Big Boss Man
Singing Tree
Just Call Me Lonesome
Guitar Man

ELVIS' GOLD RECORDS VOLUME 4 - 1968

Love Letters
Witchcraft
It Hurts Me
What'd I Say
Please Don't Drag that String Around
Indescribably Blue
Devil in Disguise
Lonely Man
A Mess of Blues
Ask Me
Ain't that Loving You Baby
Just Tell Her Jim Said Hello

SPEEDWAY

Speedway
There Ain't Nothing Like a Song
Your Time Hasn't Come Yet Baby
Who Are You
He's Your Uncle, Not Your Dad
Let Yourself Go
Your groovy self (Duet With Nancy Sinatra)
Five Sleepy Heads
Western Union
Mine
Goin' Home
Suppose

ELVIS SINGING FLAMING STAR AND OTHERS

Flaming Star
Wonderful World
Night Life
All I Needed Was the Rain
Too Much Monkey Business
The Yellow Rose of Texas/ The Eyes of Texas
She's a Machine
Do the Vega
Tiger Man

ELVIS TV SPECIAL

Trouble
Guitar Man
Lawdy Miss Clawdy
Baby, What You Want Me to Do
Heartbreak Hotel
Hound Dog
All Shook Up
Can't Help Falling in Love
Jailhouse Rock
Love Me Tender
Where Could I Go but to the Lord
Up Above My Head
Saved
Blue Christmas
One Night
Memories
Nothingville
Big Boss Man
Guitar Man
Little Egypt
Trouble
Guitar Man
If I Can Dream

FROM ELVIS IN MEMPHIS

Wearin' that Loved-on Look
Only the Strong Survive
I'll Hold You in My Heart
Long Black Limousine
It Keeps Right on A-hurtin'
I'm Movin' On
Power of My Love
Gentle on My Mind
After Loving You
True Love Travels on a Gravel Road
Any Day Now
In the Ghetto

FROM MEMPHIS TO VEGAS - FROM VEGAS TO MEMPHIS

Blue Suede Shoes
Johnny B. Good
All Shook Up
Are You Lonesome Tonight
Hound Dog
I Can't Stop Loving You
My Babe
Mystery Train/ Tiger Man
Words
In the Ghetto
Suspicious Minds
Can't Help Falling in Love

BACK IN MEMPHIS

Inherit the Wind
This Is the Story
Stranger in My Own Home Town
A Little Bit of Green
And the Grass Won't Pay No Mind
Do You Know Who I Am
From a Jack to a King
The Fair's Moving On
You'll Think of Me
Without Love

LET'S BE FRIENDS

Stay Away Joe
If I'm a Fool
Let's Be Friends
Let's Forget About the Stars
Mama
I'll Be There
Almost
Change of Habit
Have a Happy

ON STAGE

See See Rider
Release Me
Sweet Caroline
Runaway
The Wonder of You
Polk Salad Annie
Yesterday
Proud Mary
Walk a Mile in My Shoes
Let It Be Me

WORLDWIDE 50 GOLD AWARD HITS, VOL. 1

Heartbreak Hotel
I Was the One
I Want You, I Need You, I Love You
Don't Be Cruel
Hound Dog
Love Me Tender
Anyway You Want Me
Too Much
Playing for Keeps
All Shook Up
That's When Your Heartaches Begin
Loving You
Teddy Bear
Jailhouse Rock
Treat Me Nice
I Beg of You
Don't

Wear My Ring Around Your Neck
Hard Headed Woman
I Got Stung
A Fool Such as I
A Big Hunk o' Love
Stuck on You
A Mess of Blues
It's Now or Never
I Gotta Know
Are You Lonesome Tonight
Surrender
I Feel So Bad
Little Sister
Can't Help Falling in Love
Rock-a-hula Baby
Anything That's Part of You
Good Luck Charm
She's Not You
Return to Sender
Where Do You Come From
One Broken Heart for Sale
Devil in Disguise
Bossa Nova, Baby
Kissin' Cousins
Viva Las Vegas
Ain't that Loving You Baby
Wooden Heart
Crying in the Chapel
If I Can Dream
In the Ghetto
Suspicious Minds
Don't Cry Daddy
Kentucky Rain
Excerpts From The EP Elvis Sails

ALMOST IN LOVE

Almost in Love
Long Legged Girl
Edge of Reality
My Little Friend
A Little Less Conversation
Rubberneckin'
Clean up Your Own Backyard
U.S. Male
Charro
Stay Away Joe

ELVIS' CHRISTMAS ALBUM - 1970

Blue Christmas
Silent Night
White Christmas
Santa Claus Is Back in Town
I'll Be Home for Christmas
If Every Day Was Like Christmas
Here Comes Santa Claus
O Little Town of Bethlehem
Santa Bring My Baby Back to Me
Mama Liked the Roses

THAT'S THE WAY IT IS

I Just Can't Help Believin'
Twenty Days and Twenty Nights
How the Web Was Woven
Patch It Up
Mary in the Morning
You Don't Have to Say You Love Me
You've Lost that Lovin' Feelin'
I've Lost You
Just Pretend
Stranger in the Crowd
The Next Step Is Love
Bridge over Troubled Water

ELVIS COUNTRY - 1971

Snowbird
Tomorrow Never Comes
Little Cabin on the Hill
Whole Lotta Shakin' Goin' On
Funny How Time Slips Away
I Really Don't Want to Know
There Goes My Everything
It's Your Baby, You Rock It
The Fool
Faded Love
I Washed My Hands in Muddy Water
Make the World Go Away

YOU'LL NEVER WALK ALONE

You'll Never Walk Alone
Who Am I?
Let Us Pray
Peace in the Valley
We Call on Him
I Believe
It Is No Secret
Sing You Children
Take My Hand, Precious Lord

LOVE LETTERS FROM ELVIS

Love Letters
When I'm Over You
If I Were You
Got My Mojo Working
Heart of Rome
Only Believe
This Is Our Dance
Cindy, Cindy
I'll Never Know
It Ain't No Big Thing but It's Growing
Life

C'MON EVERYBODY

C'mon Everybody
Angel
Easy Come, Easy Go
A Whistling Tune
Follow that Dream
King of the Whole Wide World
I'll Take Love
Today, Tomorrow and Forever
I'm Not the Marrying Kind
This is Living

THE OTHER SIDES - WORLDWIDE GOLD AWARD HITS, VOL. 2

Puppet on a String
Witchcraft
Trouble
Poor Boy
I Want to Be Free
Doncha' Think It's Time
Young Dreams
The Next Step Is Love
You Don't Have to Say You Love Me
Paralyzed
My Wish Came True
When My Blue Moon Turns to Gold Again
Lonesome Cowboy
My Baby Left Me
It Hurts Me
I Need Your Love Tonight
Tell Me Why
Please Don't Drag that String Around
Young and Beautiful
Hot Dog
New Orleans
We're Gonna Move
Crawfish
King Creole
I Believe in the Man in the Sky
Dixieland Rock
The Wonder of You
They Remind Me Too Much of You
Mean Woman Blues
Lonely Man

Any Day Now
Don't Ask Me Why
His Latest Flame
I Really Don't Want to Know
Baby I Don't Care
I've Lost You
Let Me
Love Me
Got a Lot o' Livin' to Do
Fame and Fortune
Rip It Up
There Goes My Everything
Lover Doll
One Night
Just Tell Her Jim Said Hello
Ask Me
Patch It Up
As Long as I Have You
You'll Think of Me

I GOT LUCKY

I Got Lucky
What a Wonderful Life
I Need Somebody to Lean On
Yoga Is as Yoga Does
Riding the Rainbow
Fools Fall in Love
The Love Machine
Home Is Where the Heart Is
You Gotta Stop
If You Think I Don't Need You

ELVIS SINGS THE WONDERFUL WORLD OF CHRISTMAS

O Come, All Ye Faithful
The First Noel
On a Snowy Christmas Night
Winter Wonderland
The Wonderful World of Christmas
I'll Be Home on Christmas Day
It Won't Seem Like Christmas
If I Get Home on Christmas Day
Holly Leaves and Christmas Trees

Merry Christmas Baby
Silver Bells

ELVIS NOW 1972

Help Me Make It Through the Night
Miracle of the Rosary
Hey Jude
Put Your Hand in the Hand
Until It's Time for You to Go
We Can Make the Morning
Early Mornin' Rain
Sylvia
Fools Rush In
I Was Born About Ten Thousand Years Ago

HE TOUCHED ME

He Touched Me
I've Got Confidence
Amazing Grace
Seeing Is Believing
He Is My Everything
Bosom of Abraham
An Evening Prayer
Lead Me, Guide Me
There Is No God but God
A Thing Called Love
I, John
Reach out to Jesus

ELVIS SINGS HITS FROM HIS MOVIES, VOL. 1

Down by the Riverside and When the Saints Come
Marchin' In
They Remind Me Too Much of You
Confidence
Frankie and Johnny
Guitar Man
Long Legged Girl
You Don't Know Me
How Would You Like to Be?
Big Boss Man
Old MacDonald

ELVIS AS RECORDED AT MADISON SQUARE GARDEN

Also Sprach Zarathustra
That's All Right, Mama
Proud Mary
Never Been to Spain
You Don't Have to Say You Love Me
You've Lost that Lovin' Feelin'
Polk Salad Annie
Love Me
All Shook Up
Heartbreak Hotel
Teddy Bear/Don't Be Cruel
Love Me Tender
The Impossible Dream
Introductions by Elvis
Hound Dog
Suspicious Minds
For the Good Times
An American Trilogy
Funny How Time Slips Away
I Can't Stop Loving You
Can't Help Falling in Love

BURNING LOVE AND HITS FROM HIS MOVIES

Burning Love
Tender Feeling
Am I Ready
Tonight Is So Right for Love
Guadalajara
It's a Matter of Time
No More
Santa Lucia
We'll Be Together
I Love Only One Girl

SEPARATE WAYS

Separate Ways
Sentimental Me
In My Way
I Met Her Today
What Now, What Next, Where To
Always on My Mind
I Slipped, I Stumbled, I Fell
Is It So Strange
Forget Me Never
Old Shep

ALOHA FROM HAWAII VIA SATELLITE - 1973

Also Sprach Zarathustra
See See Rider
Burning Love
Something
You Gave Me a Mountain
Steamroller Blues
My Way
Love Me
Johnny B. Good
It's Over
Blue Suede Shoes
I'm So Lonesome I Could Cry
I Can't Stop Loving You
Hound Dog
What Now My Love
Fever
Welcome to My World
Suspicious Minds
Introductions by Elvis
I'll Remember You
Long Tall Sally
Whole Lotta Shakin' Goin' On
An American Trilogy
A Big Hunk o' Love
Can't Help Falling in Love

ELVIS (Fool)

Fool
Where Do I Go from Here
Love Me, Love the Life I Lead
It's Still Here
It's Impossible
For Lovin' Me
Padre
I'll Take You Home Again Kathleen
I Will Be True
Don't Think Twice It's All Right

RAISED ON ROCK

Raised on Rock
Are You Sincere
Find out What's Happening
I Miss You
Girl of Mine
For Ol' Times Sake
If You Don't Come Back
Just a Little Bit
Sweet Angeline
Three Corn Patches

A LEGENDARY PERFORMER, VOL. 1

That's All Right, Mama
I Love You Because
Heartbreak Hotel
Don't Be Cruel
Love Me
Tryin' to Get to You
Love Me Tender
Peace in the Valley
(Now and Then There's) A Fool Such as I
Tonight's All Right for Love
Are You Lonesome Tonight
Can't Help Falling in Love
Press Conference Excerpts

GOOD TIMES - 1974

Take Good Care of Her
Lovin' Arms
I Got a Feelin' in My Body
If that Isn't Love
She Wears My Ring
I've Got a Thing about You Baby
My Boy
Spanish Eyes
Talk about the Good Times
Good Time Charlie's Got the Blues

ELVIS AS RECORDED LIVE ON STAGE IN MEMPHIS

See See Rider
I Got a Woman
Love Me
Tryin' to Get to You
Long Tall Sally
Whole Lotta Shakin' Goin' On
Mama Don't Dance
Flip, Flop and Fly
Jailhouse Rock
Hound Dog
Why Me Lord
How Great Thou Art
Blueberry Hill
I Can't Stop Loving You
Help Me
An American Trilogy
Let Me Be There
My Baby Left Me
Lawdy Miss Clawdy
Can't Help Falling in Love
Closing Vamp

HAVING FUN WITH ELVIS ON STAGE

Talking only album

PROMISED LAND

Promised Land
There's a Honky Tonk Angel
Help Me
Mr. Songman
Love Song of the Year
It's Midnight
Your Love's Been a Long Time Coming
If You Talk in Your Sleep
Thinking about You
You Asked Me To

PURE GOLD

Kentucky Rain
Fever
It's Impossible
Jailhouse Rock
Don't Be Cruel
I Got a Woman
All Shook Up
Loving You
In the Ghetto
Love Me Tender

TODAY

T-R-O-U-B-L-E
And I Love You So
Susan When She Tried
Woman Without Love
Shake a Hand
Pieces of My Life
Fairytale
I Can Help
Bringin' It Back
Green Green Grass of Home

A LEGENDARY PERFORMER, VOL. 2

Harbor Lights
Interview With Elvis
How Great Thou Art
If I Can Dream

I Want You, I Need You, I Love You
Blue Suede Shoes
Blue Christmas
Jailhouse Rock
It's Now or Never
A Cane and a High Starched Collar
Presentation of Awards to Elvis
Blue Hawaii
Such a Night
Baby, What You Want Me to Do
How Great Thou Art
If I Can Dream

THE SUN SESSIONS

That's All Right, Mama
Blue Moon of Kentucky
I Don't Care if the Sun Don't Shine
Good Rockin' Tonight
Milkcow Blues Boogie
You're a Heartbreaker
I'm Left, You're Right, She's Gone
Baby, Let's Play House
Mystery Train
I Forgot to Remember to Forget
I'll Never Let You Go
I Love You Because
Tryin' to Get to You
Blue Moon
Just Because
I Love You Because (Take 2)

FROM ELVIS PRESLEY BOULEVARD, MEMPHIS, TENNESSEE

Hurt
Never Again
Blue Eyes Crying in the Rain
Danny Boy
The Last Farewell
For the Heart
Bitter They Are, Harder They Fall
Solitaire
Love Coming Down
I'll Never Fall in Love Again

WELCOME TO MY WORLD - 1977

Welcome to My World
Help Me Make It Through the Night
Release Me
I Really Don't Want to Know
For the Good Times
Make the World Go Away
Gentle on My Mind
I'm So Lonesome I Could Cry
Your Cheatin' Heart
I Can't Stop Loving You

MOODY BLUE

Unchained Melody
If You Love Me
Little Darlin'
He'll Have to Go
Let Me Be There
Way Down
Pledging My Love
Moody Blue
She Thinks I Still Care
It's Easy for You

ELVIS IN CONCERT

Elvis Fans' Comments / Opening Riff
Also Sprach Zarathustra
See See Rider
That's All Right, Mama
Are You Lonesome Tonight
Teddy Bear
Don't Be Cruel
Elvis Fans' Comments
You Gave Me a Mountain
Jailhouse Rock
Elvis Fans' Comments
How great Thou art
Elvis Fans' Comments
I Really Don't Want to Know
Elvis Introduces His Father
Hurt
Hound Dog
My Way
Can't Help Falling in Love
Closing Riff
Special Message from Elvis' Father
I Got a Woman/Amen
Elvis Talks
Love Me
If You Love Me
O Sole Mio (Sherrill Nielsen)
It's Now or Never
Tryin' to Get to You
Hawaiian Wedding Song
Fairytale
Little Sister
Early Mornin' Rain
What'd I Say
Johnny B. Good
And I Love You So